Hand Of Fate

The Hand Of Westerns
Book 1

By
Duane Boehm

Hand Of Fate

ISBN: 9781687366740

Other Books by Duane Boehm

In Just One Moment
Gideon Johann: A Gideon Johann Western Prequel
Last Stand: A Gideon Johann Western Book 1
Last Chance: A Gideon Johann Western Book 2
Last Hope: A Gideon Johann Western Book 3
Last Ride: A Gideon Johann Western Book 4
Last Breath: A Gideon Johann Western Book 5
Last Journey: A Gideon Johann Western Book 6
Last Atonement: A Gideon Johann Western Book 7
*Wayward Brother: A Gideon Johann Western
Book 8*
*Where The Wild Horses Run: Wild Horse Westerns
Book 1*
*Spirit Of The Wild Horse: Wild Horse Westerns
Book 2*
*Wild Horse On The Run: Wild Horse Westerns
Book 3*
What It All Comes Down To
Hand Of The Father: The Hand Of Westerns Book 2
Trail To Yesterday
Sun Over The Mountains
*Wanted: A Collection of Western Stories (7
authors)*
*Wanted II: A Collection of Western Stories (7
authors)*

Dedicated to Karen Holt and those years of sharing an office

Chapter 1

Flannery Vogel arose at the crack of dawn to head to the barn so that her two-year-old daughter Savannah would have fresh milk for breakfast. She grabbed a shawl hanging on a peg on the wall and threw it over her shoulders to ward off the coolness of the May morning. A cautious woman by nature, she grabbed the Winchester '73 hanging above the door before venturing outside the home.

When Flannery walked into the barn, an audible gasp escaped her at the sight of a man sleeping in a pile of straw. The sound of her chambering a cartridge into the rifle stirred the vagrant from his sleep and he clumsily jumped to his feet.

"Don't shoot. I mean no harm," he pleaded, and raised his hands in the air.

"What are you doing in here?" Flannery screamed as she shouldered her Winchester and put a bead on the intruder. She was in such a panic that her heart felt as if it might pound right through her chest. In the dim light, she frantically tried to take in all of the man's features in hopes that she might recognize him, all to no avail.

"I arrived here in the middle of the night and figured that knocking on the door at that hour just might get me shot, so I thought I'd sleep in your barn until morning."

"That still doesn't answer my question."

"Oh – I guess it doesn't. I'm Boone Youngblood. I'm a friend of Jimmy's. He can vouch for me."

Flannery narrowed her eyes and squeezed her lips so tightly together that they all but disappeared. She'd heard the name Boone Youngblood before, but still had her doubts that this could really be the man standing in front of her. From what she could see, his shoddy appearance didn't fit the picture she had in her mind of him. "How did you know where to find this place?" she asked.

"Jimmy brought me here years ago before he even owned the land. After all those years in Texas, he loved the green of Colorado. He vowed he'd own this place someday, and then he planned to head back to Vicksburg to marry you. I never doubted him for a minute. Oh, I hope I didn't just misspeak. You are Flannery, aren't you?"

Overcome with relief that Boone Youngblood knew too much information not to be the man he said he was, Flannery's shoulders began trembling as she pointed the rifle toward the ground and gently released the hammer. "Mr. Youngblood, I'm afraid I have some bad news," she said, her southern drawl much more apparent now that she wasn't speaking in a panic. "Jimmy has been dead for two years now."

Boone seemed to wilt right before Flannery's eyes. He dropped onto his butt in the straw and covered his face with his hands. No sound escaped him but his whole body shook. Surprised by his actions, Flannery stood uncomfortably, switching her weight from one foot to the other as she watched on.

He finally dropped his hands from his face and looked up at her. "I'm so sorry for your loss. I swear to you that I never heard the news."

Flannery still wasn't thrilled with having found Boone in her barn, but she did feel a smidgen of compassion for him. Jimmy had clearly meant a great deal to the young man. "Jimmy spoke highly of you. I'm sure this has been quite a shock. I don't imagine word of his death traveled far. It's not like we're of any notoriety."

"What happened?"

"Somebody shot him. I don't know who did it. There are a couple of ranchers that's had it in for us ever since Jimmy bought this place out from under their noses."

"Ma'am, I know I'm not much of anything to look at right now, but there was a time when I was somebody, and I owe that all to Jimmy. He made a man out of me. I'm truly grieving," Boone said. He took his shirtsleeve and wiped it across his face.

"Are you hungry?"

"I haven't eaten since the day before yesterday. I'm about half starved."

"Let me milk the cow while you collect yourself, and then you can have breakfast with us," Flannery said. She grabbed a bucket and walked into a stall.

By the time Flannery finished milking the cow, Boone had regained his composure. He slung the knapsack with his meager possessions over his shoulder and then took the bucket from Flannery as they began walking out of the barn. The sun had risen enough by that time that she could finally get a good look at the unexpected visitor. Her first impression was that most women would consider Boone to be handsome with his strong chin and high cheekbones even if he looked dirty and poorly dressed. He was of average height and thin with mousey-brown hair and dark piercing eyes. While his features favored those of a white man, his dark complexion gave the notion that he might have some Mexican or Indian in his blood. His pants had holes in the knees and his shirt was about two sizes too big. He didn't even wear a gun or hat. His boots were the only thing about him that were of good quality and condition.

Flannery was surprised by the appearance of Boone. While Jimmy had talked little of his days as a Texas Ranger, when he did, he had always spoken of the young man with a real fondness and admiration. He had also joked on occasion about Boone's persnickety detail to dress, and of his vanity. No one would certainly ever accuse Boone of such a thing now.

Boone tried to get a good look at Flannery, too, without being obvious. She was tall for a woman and too skinny. She might have been pretty if she had a little meat on her bones, but her chin and cheekbones looked as if at any moment they might cut through her gaunt and sunburned face, and her mouth gave the appearance that life had molded it into a permanent frown with only her dark auburn hair and pretty blue eyes softening her features.

Back in the day when the Rangers would sit around a campfire at night, Jimmy would wax on to Boone and the other men about his girl back in Vicksburg. From his descriptions, Flannery was the prettiest Southern belle to ever draw breath below the Mason-Dixon Line. He would talk of how she survived the siege of Vicksburg as a child with her dignity and humor still intact, and of her love of pranks and dancing. If Jimmy had been telling the truth, Boone figured his death and some hard years had robbed her of all those traits.

When Boone and Flannery entered the house, he was surprised to see an older black woman cooking breakfast and a small child sitting in a highchair. The little girl looked up at Boone and smiled, giving him a moment of recognition that sent him reeling back in time and made the death of Jimmy even keener. She definitely had her daddy's grin as well as his curly blond hair and blue eyes.

"Jenny, we have a guest for breakfast. I'm sure you remember Jimmy talking about Boone Youngblood. He decided to pay us a visit," Flannery said.

The black woman looked Boone up and down, and didn't smile or offer a greeting. If anything, she had a look of contempt for the visitor. "Yes, Flannery, whatever you say," she said before turning back toward the stove.

"Mr. Youngblood, there is soap at the sink. You can scrub there, if you like," Flannery said.

Boone looked down at his dirty hands and at the grime under his fingernails. At that moment, he became painfully aware of his appearance. "Thank you. You can call me Boone, please," he said.

While Boone scrubbed his hands and face, he felt eyes upon him and turned to see Jenny staring his way as she stirred the eggs. Her expression toward him had certainly not softened, leaving no doubt that she didn't appreciate his intruding upon the home.

After drying off his hands and face, Boone said, "I apologize for my appearance. I've had a run of bad luck lately and this is what I have to show for it." He made a sweep of his hand, pointing toward his attire.

"We've all been there," Flannery said in an attempt to ease Boone's discomfort. "By the way, this here is Savannah."

Boone walked over to the child and placed his hand on her shoulder. "Hello, Savannah. Nice to meet you." The little girl made him feel nostalgic for Jimmy, and touching her gave him the sense that he had somehow connected with his dead friend.

"Hi," Savannah said and smiled at Boone again.

The notion came to Boone that Jimmy may have never gotten to see his daughter before his death. That thought only added to his grief and made his chest ache. He had to know the answer to his fear. "Did Jimmy live to see her born?" he asked.

The question caught Flannery by surprise and knocked her from her reverie concerning her daughter. "The news of Jimmy's death sent me into early labor. I lost him and had Savannah all in the same day. I don't know what I would have done if Jenny hadn't taken care of us. Those days are all kind of a blur."

"Again, I'm so sorry for your loss. That must make for a bad and joyous day all at the same time. I can't imagine. This sure isn't what I expected."

Jenny brought a bowl of scrambled eggs, bacon, biscuits, and gravy to the table. "Best get to eating 'fore the food gets cold," she said in an icy tone.

Flannery cut her eyes at the old woman. "Well, then by all means, let's eat."

Boone felt so hungry that he had to remind himself not make a spectacle out of his eating. He paced his bites and chewed the food methodically so as not to seem as if he was rushing.

The conversation lagged and made for an uncomfortable silence. To end the stillness, Flannery said, "Jimmy never mentioned how you two met. Maybe you can enlighten us."

With a nervous laugh, Boone grinned sheepishly and glanced down at his plate for a moment before looking up. "I was playing poker with him in Amarillo, and I was cheating. Jimmy called me out, and me being young and a hothead, I jumped up and started to draw my gun. Jimmy shoved the table into me and knocked me off-balance. He stood and drew his revolver. We were both standing there pointing our guns at each other. To this day, I don't know what kept either of us from shooting the other one. Jimmy said, 'You can either die young at some card table in Texas or you can change your ways and I'll show you how to use that gun for something bigger than yourself.' I took him up on his offer and I've never cheated again since that day. I was already good with a gun, but I was green as all get-out. Jimmy kept me alive and taught me how to fight until I finally made a respectable Ranger. I never did figure out what made him decide to take me under his wing after such an unpleasant introduction. And like I already said, he made a man out of me."

Flannery nodded her head, her eyes glistening. "That sounds like my Jimmy."

"He certainly was a good man, and I still can't believe he's gone. Jimmy always seemed to me to be bigger than life itself. So what all happened here?"

"Jimmy purchased this 2,000-acre ranch after he left the Rangers, and built the house and barn before he came back to Vicksburg to marry me. When Joseph Thurgood and Wendell Starr found out he bought this place, they weren't pleased. They're the two biggest ranchers around Trinidad. They gave him some trouble, but nothing to worry ourselves over. Jimmy was always good with money and we had enough to buy a cattle herd to get started. We were happy and things were going well, but the better we did, the more trouble we had, and then the threats began. One day, Jimmy was out with the herd and somebody shot him. Jenny and I have managed to keep things going the best we can."

Boone shook his head in disgust. His face had colored and his piercing eyes looked as if they could bore holes through a wall. "That's a lowdown thing to do, especially when you were carrying a child. Don't you have some ranch hands to help you?"

"They scared off all of them. I go to town and hire some drunks for a few days when I really need help."

"Have they threatened you?"

"No, they leave us alone. I'm guessing they're waiting for me to fail so they don't look as if they're going after a woman. They probably plan to fight it out amongst themselves if that day were to come."

The conversation stalled and everyone ate in silence until Savannah struck up a conversation with Boone. The child was quite verbal for her age, and peppered him with questions about his name, where he came from, and anything else that came to her young mind. Boone good-naturedly answered her inquiries. He found her command of English to be amazing and her personality was nothing short of precocious.

As Boone finished the last of his biscuits and gravy, Flannery set her fork down and placed her palms on the table. "Boone, why did you come to see Jimmy?" she asked.

Boone let out a sigh that sounded as if the weight of the world sat on his shoulders. He looked Flannery in the eye before speaking. "As you can see, I'm down on my luck. I came here hoping that Jimmy could put me up and give me a job until I got back on my feet. I didn't have anywhere else to turn."

"How did you get in such shape?"

"Ma'am, I like to play poker. I've had the worst streak of cards you'll ever see in your life. I've lost my horse, my guns, and even my suit. It's like nothing I've ever seen."

"I would think one would quit before he lost everything he owned. Maybe you're just not very good at cards," Flannery said.

Flannery's audacity rubbed Boone the wrong way, and he didn't appreciate her speculating on his skills at playing poker.

"I've done plenty of winning in my day, and against some of the best, but sometimes you can't get a word in edgewise with lady luck, but you're right in that I should have known when to quit," he said.

The tone of Boone's words made Flannery realize she had hit a raw nerve. Her directness had served her well many times in her life, but she didn't wish to alienate Jimmy's friend. "I know nothing of cards. I should have held my opinions to myself. My apologies."

"That's all right. I didn't come here to discuss cards anyway. I need a job and it seems to me that you need help. How do you feel about such an arrangement?"

At a loss for words, Flannery glanced at Jenny. She had expected Boone would move on without being so bold as to ask for work now that he knew of Jimmy's death.

Jenny stood up and began clearing the dishes. "Young man, you got your belly full, and now you need to leave. We might not be doing well, but we're getting by. You'll just bring more trouble down on us," she said.

Boone wasn't sure if he was more surprised that Jenny finally spoke to him or that Flannery had let the old woman do the talking. He stood and pushed his chair into place at the table. "That's fine if I'm not welcome here, but I'll be in Trinidad. I'll get me a job and sleep in an alley if I have to until I make some money. One way or the other though, I'm going to look out for your interests."

Flannery jumped up from her seat, banging her knee into the table leg as she did so and causing her to wince and the dishes to rattle. She moved around the table to be next to Jenny as if to suggest strength in numbers. "Mr. Youngblood, I don't know why you would think that the man I found sleeping in my barn this morning would be someone that I would want looking out for me. I've seen beggars dressed better than you. Your appearance and current situation doesn't exactly fill me with confidence in your abilities in much of anything. I think you should take your leave now." Her voice sounded loud and harsh.

Savannah started to cry, scared by her mother's outburst. Jenny had her hands full of dishes and Flannery had moved to the other side of the table from her daughter. Boone scooped Savannah from her highchair and held her to his chest. He began patting the youngster's back and talking to her in a soothing tone. His actions so surprised the women that they stood there awestruck.

When Savannah quieted down, Boone looked at Flannery and said in a calm voice, "I'm sorry to have upset everyone. That wasn't my intention. I'll leave now, but I want you to know that if not for Jimmy, I'd be God knows where. I might not look like much now, but I'll get back on my feet. Jimmy taught me how to live an honorable life. And if the tables were turned, Jimmy would have done everything under the sun for my family. I'm going to do the same for you whether you like it or not. I have to do that for my friend – I just have to. I couldn't live with myself otherwise." He passed Savannah to her mother and turned to leave.

"Boone, please take a seat," Flannery said.

Boone turned and looked at the women before sitting back down in his chair. Jenny looked as if she would have liked to take Flannery to the woodshed, but Flannery did make a halfhearted attempt to smile at him.

"You look like you and Jimmy are about the same size. Jenny and I will go here in a minute and find you some clothes and a hat to wear. There's a creek out back with a nice pool in it. After we get you your clothes, you can take some soap out there and scrub up. There's no call for uncleanliness."

Boone nodded his head.

"But those are Jimmy's clothes," Jenny protested.

Flannery made a little shake of her head. "Jimmy certainly isn't going to be wearing them any longer," she said.

Chapter 2

As soon as Joseph Thurgood and his youngest son, Elliot, neared the barn, Joseph's other two sons, Hunter and Logan, knew their old man must be in an ornery mood. His eyes were narrowed and looked like two flaming coals, and his jaw thrust forward with a scowl on his lips. Hunter and Logan exchanged glances, wondering which one of them had caused the ire of their old man this time.

The two older sons had their own homes because of their father's temperament. To escape his wrath, they'd both moved out of their parents' house as soon as they had finished their schooling. Hunter had since married and had two children while Logan remained a bachelor.

Joseph looked around and saw too many ranch hands lingering in earshot range. "We need to go in the house and talk," he said. He turned around and began walking back toward his home without waiting for reactions from his sons. His strides were with purpose and long for his short stocky frame.

The sons followed their father to the house and into his study. He shut the door and took a seat behind his massive walnut desk that he'd had shipped in from Pennsylvania.

"Take seats. I don't feel like staring at your crotches," Joseph said. He waited to speak until his sons were all seated. "We have a problem. Wendell Starr finally bullied Anderson Clark into selling him his place at half what it's worth. Word is he gave Anderson a choice to sell or die. If we don't get off our asses, Wendell is going to own this whole county."

Silence hung in the air with enough tension to cut with a knife as the sons waited each other out to be the first to speak. Experience had taught them that no matter what was said, the response would be met with disdain.

"What do you propose we do about it?" Logan finally asked.

Joseph slapped his desk. "I say we need to start doing more of the same. When is the last time we ran off one of these small-time dreamers? We've gotten soft," he roared.

"Pa, how much more land do we need? With the open range land, we have all the ground we need for our herds," Logan said.

"If that isn't just like you to never see into the future. Someday, there won't be any open range. All of the land will be owned. We need to acquire all of it that we can. I'll be damned if I'll sit by and let Wendell grab up all of it."

Hunter leaned forward in his chair. Of the three sons, he looked the most like his father, and his dour expression only added to the resemblance. "Where do you want to begin?"

"I say we go after Flannery Vogel. I'm tired of waiting for that widow to give up. I'll say one thing about her though – she's got some grit to last as long as she has without a crew."

Logan popped the arms of his leather-covered chair. "We're distrusted in town enough the way it is. If we go messing with Flannery, we're liable to drive everyone into Wendell's camp. They may have no use for him, too, but going after a woman will be the final straw."

Elliot let out a snicker. "What's the matter? Are you sweet on the widow?"

Joseph stared at his youngest son. "My God, you're twenty-one years old. Can't you ever act your age instead of parading around like some idiot schoolboy?"

The rebuke caused Elliot to fold his arms and turn sullen.

Next, Hunter took his shot at Logan. "You always were soft and afraid to get a little blood on your hands. This land got built by those willing to fight for it."

"This isn't the days of killing off the Indians like they were nothing better than varmints. We can't go around murdering people for their land. No good can come from it and there will come a day of reckoning," Logan said.

"There you go crying about the poor Indians again. You're an Indian lover. We wouldn't be here now if they weren't whipped. You have to look at it as if we're in a war with the other ranchers. People die in wars," Hunter said.

"That's ridiculous. Someone may have gotten by with killing Jimmy Vogel, but that won't always be the case," Logan said.

Joseph exchanged glances with Hunter. The gesture didn't go unnoticed by Logan.

Logan looked at his brother and then toward his father. "You promised me that you didn't kill Jimmy. Did you lie to me? It's a funny thing that I've never heard a single rumor on who did it. Usually, some ranch hand will get drunk and start bragging about his exploits. Nobody has claimed to have had a hand in Jimmy's death."

"I told you we didn't have anything to do with that. Now don't bring it up again. I gave you my word," Joseph said.

Hunter jumped to his feet. "Let's go pay the widow a visit."

"Sit back down. I don't pay you to think," Joseph yelled. "Logan does have a good point about rousing the townsfolk. The Vogel widow has some prime land along the river, but it's not worth stirring up Trinidad over right now. Let's go pay Simon Cruft a visit instead."

"Pa, you know that old Englishman can't be scared off," Logan objected. "If you go there, you'll just be making an enemy. He's never done us wrong."

Joseph leaned back in his chair and folded his hands upon his chest as he studied his son. "The trouble with you is that you're too much like your mother. You read too many books and philosophize all the time. It makes you soft like her. I'm afraid you just don't understand how the world works. Go on and get the ranch hands busy. Hunter and Elliot will help me with Simon."

Logan stared back at his father and didn't speak for a long moment. "I'm telling you this is a mistake. You'll bring disgrace to our family."

"Go on and get out of here."

Logan lifted his long lanky frame out of the chair. He had inherited his height and good looks from his mother's side of the family, and stood a head higher than his father and brothers. Much to Joseph's chagrin, he'd often been teased that Logan must be one of the ranch hand's sons. Logan rushed out of the study without saying another word.

Joseph waited until he heard Logan slam the door on his way out of the house before he spoke again. "Let's go find Simon. I'll do all the talking. You boys follow my lead. Don't either of you simpletons do something stupid. You two may have grit unlike your delicate brother, but he's the only one of you with any brains. Now it's time to go."

The men walked out of the house and saddled their horses. Simon Cruft's place sat to the east and they headed in that direction. The Cruft ranch was a 5,000-acre spread of prime grassland that abutted the Thurgood ranch, and would take an hour to reach. After they crossed the Purgatoire River, they rode in its shallow edge for three miles to avoid leaving tracks in case it would become necessary to avoid being tracked.

"What are we going to do if Simon won't sell?" Hunter asked as they left the water.

"You let me worry about that," Joseph replied.

"Simon is a pretty big man in these here parts. Aren't you worried we'll stir up a hornet's nest if we kill him?"

Joseph glanced over at his son and shook his head. "You're starting to sound like Logan now. That old bachelor doesn't have any family. Nobody will care if he's gone. You need to trust me on this."

"But we'll still have to outbid Wendell for the land if we kill Simon."

"Damn, boy, you're worrying a lot today. Wendell will be stretched thin after buying Clark's place. I'll have me a little talk with the bank. I can convince Oscar Hamilton not to give Wendell any more credit," Joseph said. He smiled and gave his son a wink.

Once they had crossed onto Cruft's land, finding him would be their next challenge. They finally spotted some men off in the distance. Joseph pulled his spyglass from his saddlebag and studied the scene. The men were busy branding the new calves born that spring.

Simon was known to ride a tall white horse, and was nowhere to be seen.

"He's not with them. Let's keep riding," Joseph said.

Another hour passed as they searched across the ranch. They finally rode up a large hill to gain the view of the valley below them and saw three men riding amongst a herd of cattle. The sunlight reflecting off Simon's white horse made for easy identification of the rancher.

"This is better than I expected. I thought we'd be dealing with more ranch hands. We'll see how this goes. Maybe Simon will be ready to sell," Joseph said. He nudged his horse into moving toward the rancher.

Simon glanced away from the herd and spotted the Thurgoods riding his way. "Joseph, what brings you clear over this way?" he called out in his thick English accent that hadn't softened a bit in the twenty years since he'd left his native England.

"Can't a neighbor pay a visit? How are the cattle looking?" Joseph asked as Simon's two ranch hands rode up beside their boss.

"The herd is looking fine. I'm pleased with the calves sired by those Hereford bulls I imported from the mother country, too. I believe they may be the future of the cattle herds out here. They seem to adapt to this land quite well."

"That's good to hear and know. Simon, I'm just going to get right to the point of why I'm here. The reason I came today is that I've been thinking that you're getting to the age where maybe you would want to slow down or do some traveling. I'd like to buy your spread and herd. I'll keep all your ranch hands and at their same pay. You can even stay in the house until you die. Hell,

I'll even bury you in the yard if you like," Joseph said, ending with a friendly laugh.

Simon let out a little chuckle. "Joseph, men like you and I wouldn't know what to do with ourselves if we were to retire. We'd probably sit in a chair and waste away in no time. Working is in our blood and the only thing we know. I plan to drop dead in the saddle while checking on my herd."

"Don't you want to take some time to even consider it?"

"I suspect you are feeling threatened after Wendell bought out Anderson Clark's ranch. Joseph, you have nothing to worry about. You and your boys run a much better operation than Wendell ever thought about having. Wendell will spread himself too thin and get into difficulties. You'll outlive me by a good bit. Buy my place after I die."

Joseph glanced to his left at his son Elliot and then to his right toward Hunter. He made an almost imperceptible nod of his head. "Oh, I'm going to buy your place for sure. I'm also going to grant your wish to die in the saddle," he said. He drew his revolver and shot Simon in the chest at pointblank.

Before Simon's ranch hands could react from the shock of seeing their boss gunned down, Elliot and Hunter shot them. One of the men flopped backward onto the rump of his horse and the other slumped forward onto the horse's neck.

Simon grasped his chest, looking at the Thurgood family in disbelief. He opened his mouth to speak, but before a word escaped him, Joseph shot him in the head.

"Put a shot into their heads and let's get the hell out of here," Joseph ordered.

The brothers did as instructed, and the family took off in a hard lope to escape their crimes. They headed straight for the river, and upon reaching it, they again rode into the shallow water before heading toward their ranch.

Logan was helping mend fence when he saw his family riding hard toward the house. He gave the ranch hands orders to keep working while he mounted his horse and rode home. His father and brothers were unsaddling their lathered horses as he arrived at the barn.

"Looks like you all were in a mighty big hurry to get back here," Logan said. He climbed down from his horse and walked over to his family.

"Pa killed Simon," Elliot said proudly.

"Damn it, Elliot, shut the hell up," Joseph warned.

Logan bent down his head, shaking it as he cupped his hand to his forehead. "Good God, I thought you'd come to your senses as you rode there. Damn, Pa, you've ruined us and apt to have started a range war. Simon was well-liked by his men. They're liable to come over here and kill us all. And do you really think the sheriff won't be suspicious that it was us? He'll probably track you right back to here."

"That sheriff won't track us anywhere. Quit your worrying. Everything will be just fine," Joseph said.

"No, it is not fine. Nothing will ever be fine again. We're nothing more than outlaws now," Logan screamed.

"Don't you talk to Pa that way," Hunter warned.

"Oh, shut up. You won't be so proud of yourself when the noose is around your neck and they're about to pull the lever. You'll be wondering why in the hell you ever thought killing Simon was a good idea."

"At least I'll die loyal to my family," Hunter yelled before tackling Logan.

The brothers wrestled in the dirt. Logan had an advantage with his long arms and legs, but Hunter was a stout man. Neither could gain the upper hand as they rolled around on the ground.

"Help me separate them before they come to blows," Joseph hollered at Elliot.

Elliot grabbed Hunter and began pulling while Joseph wrapped Logan in a headlock.

"Enough, and I mean it. I'll not have a family feud. We don't always have to agree with each other, but we will not turn on one another. Do I make myself clear?" Joseph asked.

Logan was the first to nod his head. Hunter still glared at his brother, but after his father gave him a threatening look, he made a single nod.

"Dust yourselves off. We need to tend to our horses. Then we'll go see what your momma has fixed us for lunch. Afterward, we'll get back to work as if nothing has happened. In fact, I think we'll move some cattle over our tracks to the river just to be cautious," Joseph said before looking toward Elliot. "And you boys remember to keep your mouths shut about this to everyone."

Chapter 3

Boone had insisted on helping Flannery with the chores before he bathed. While feeding the horses, he had noticed that the stalls were in need of a good cleaning. Flannery offered little resistance when he grabbed a scoop shovel and began the backbreaking task. While he scooped the manure, she wheelbarrowed it away. Most of the morning was gone by the time they finished and he headed toward the creek.

A bath, shave, and some decent clothes transformed Boone into a respectable-looking citizen. As he rinsed the shaving soap out of the washbasin, he noticed that Jenny and Savannah had disappeared from sight. Flannery sat at the table and sipped coffee as if she was waiting on him to finish cleaning up.

"I feel like a new man," Boone said as he turned to face Flannery.

"Well, I must admit that you look like one, too. I might not have had the daylights scared out of me this morning if you looked as you do now."

With a little laugh, Boone nodded his head.

"Why don't you have a seat?" Flannery asked.

Boone sat down across from her. "What is it?"

"Jenny and I talked and we've decided that you can stay in the bunkhouse. She's cleaning it now. I'm not a rich woman, but I can pay you. Honestly, we need the help if we're going to survive. I just hope you being here doesn't start trouble. You have to understand that you could be in danger."

Ignoring the warning, Boone leaned back in his chair and looked at Flannery. She certainly was a direct woman, but she was being friendlier than he had any right to expect after their inauspicious introduction. "So did Jenny really agree that I should stay?"

Flannery let out a little chuckle. "Let's just say that it took some persuasion on my part to convince her, but she came around."

"I'm betting you just put your foot down. Did she used to be your slave and you just kept her around to help?"

The question caused an instant change in Flannery's disposition. She straightened her posture and pulled her shoulders back while her blue eyes seemed to turn a steely color and her mouth became more severe-looking than ever. "This is 1880. I would think you are aware that slavery ended a long time ago. In fact, I'm sure you know that Jimmy fought in the last two years of that war. Jenny never was a slave. Her parents bought their freedom years before the war. At one point, that used to be possible in Mississippi. Jenny's momma was a wonderful seamstress and used to make dresses and such for my mother. As you can imagine, there wasn't a lot of opportunities for a free black girl. Jenny came to work for us when she came of age. She was there on the day I was born. After Jimmy and I married, Momma and Daddy felt better about me leaving for Colorado with Jenny coming out here with us. Thank God, they did. I would have never survived without Jenny."

"So Jenny basically gave up her life for your family."

The accusation only further inflamed Flannery. She jumped up from her seat and paced in front of the table a couple of times before spinning toward Boone. It seemed to her that for a man down on his luck and wanting a job, Boone sure didn't lack for opinions. "You're awfully high and mighty for someone that doesn't have a cent to their name. I fully admit that Jenny never had the opportunities of a white woman, but we certainly never made her stay. She used to have callers, but nothing ever came of them. Do you want the job or not?"

"I do. And I'm sorry I offended you. I shouldn't have been so judgmental."

"Never mind. I just want you to understand that I don't want you causing trouble with the other ranchers. We're going to try to live in harmony with them if at all possible."

"Understood."

"Come with me."

Flannery led Boone to a large wardrobe and retrieved a holstered revolver from inside it. She handed the gun to him. "You can use this and the Winchester above the door until you can buy your own guns. They both could probably use a good cleaning. I'll start carrying the shotgun when I need a weapon."

Boone pulled the revolver from the holster. The gun was one of the new Colts that used the .44-40 cartridges. Jimmy had apparently purchased it after he and Boone had parted ways. "I'll take good care of them. That's a promise." He walked over to the door and pulled down the Winchester. A smile came to him as he looked at the gun. "I was with him on the day this buttstock got that dent in it. We ran out of bullets and had to use our rifles as clubs. I didn't think we were going to get out of there with our hair still on our heads that day."

"Jimmy never liked to talk much about his days as a Texas Ranger. Maybe over time, you can fill me in with some stories."

"I just might do that. I can keep a little part of Jimmy alive that way. I guess I had better go help Jenny clean up the bunkhouse. Maybe I can begin to win her over with a little scrubbing," Boone said and chuckled. He returned the rifle to above the entrance and strapped on the revolver before opening the door to leave the home.

"Boone, just a moment, please. I know today's news has been a shock and you haven't received the warmest of welcomes, but I want you to know that you meant a lot to Jimmy. He would speculate on your whereabouts from time to time. I could tell he missed you."

"Thank you. That's good to know. I sure missed him, too. We had us some fine times together. I would imagine that he would have gotten a good laugh if he knew I was a gambler."

"Let's go help Jenny."

They found Jenny busy with dusting while Savannah sat on a bed and played with a doll. The bunkhouse had been unattended since the last ranch hand had quit, but remained in good condition and only needed to be wiped down and swept out. Flannery began helping Jenny while Boone grabbed a broom and swept.

Savannah climbed down from the bed and started following Boone. The child had had almost no interactions with males in her short life, but wasn't fazed in the least by the new guest. She peppered him with questions and got in his way.

Flannery watched her daughter with fascination. While Savannah had never met anyone she considered a stranger, her acceptance of Boone into their home still surprised her. Flannery secretly wished that she could be as comfortable in the company of strangers as her daughter. "Savannah, get out of Mr. Boone's way so he can sweep."

"Boone is my new friend," Savannah announced.

"Mr. Boone," Flannery corrected.

Ignoring her mother's directive, Savannah said, "Boone's going to play with me when he's done."

In an attempt to prevent the child from getting into trouble, Boone said, "If it's all right with you, I'd just as soon she called me Boone. I'm too young to be a mister."

"Suit yourself. I guess you should be called what you like," Flannery responded.

Jenny turned toward Boone and placed her hands on her hips. "Don't be going and spoiling our child. She'll need her good manners long after you're gone and she forgets you ever existed. Changing clothes don't change the man."

Boone could feel his ears turning red. The old woman had pushed him about as far as he planned on being pushed. Not wishing to upset Savannah, he hid his anger from sounding in his voice. "I realize I didn't make a good first impression and that you don't know me from Adam, but you have talked down to me about as much as I'm going to tolerate. I was Jimmy's friend, and not only do you disrespect me, but you disrespect him when you act as if he consorted with some villain. Regardless of what you may think, I am an honorable man and I will do nothing to cause embarrassment or harm to Jimmy's family. On that you have my word. Now you can change your tone toward me or do not speak to me again."

Jenny threw her hands into the air before turning away without saying a word. She started dusting as if she was trying to rub the finish off the wood. Flannery watched on in bemusement, stifling a smile. Rare was the occasion when Jenny didn't have the last word, but she'd already lost two battles that day. First, when Flannery had insisted that Boone would stay, and just now. The day had certainly been an interesting one so far and had actually taken Flannery's mind off the constant worry on how they would continue to survive on the ranch.

By the time they finished cleaning, the time was well past noon. Jenny stalked off to make a late lunch without so much as having said another word since her encounter with Boone.

"Will I have to worry about her coming over here and killing me in my sleep?" he asked.

Flannery smiled. "No, once she sees that you really do mean well, she'll come around. Jenny is a loyal friend when she's on your side."

In actuality, Boone had figured out as much regarding Jenny. His real concern was Flannery. While she had certainly been friendlier than Jenny, the woman had such a wall of solitariness and sadness built up around her that Boone feared it would cause her to run him off before he had a chance to help her. He didn't really care if he came to like her or Jenny, but one way or the other, he would help them for Jimmy's sake. He at least owed his old friend that much.

"While we were cleaning the stalls, I noticed some fine riding horses in your stable. Would you like to show me the ranch later?" Boone asked.

"I can do that after we have lunch."

"I go," Savannah said.

Without thinking, Boone said, "Sure, you can ride in the saddle with me."

Flannery raised her eyebrows and pursed her lips. "Savannah has never been on horseback."

"Don't worry. I'm certainly a good enough rider that I can hold a child without any problem. She'll be fine."

"That's not the point. I should be the one making the decision on whether she goes or not. I am her mother."

"Please, Momma," Savannah pleaded.

"What would it hurt?" Boone asked. "A little sunshine would be good for the child."

Flannery let out a sigh as she looked down at her daughter. "All right, this time, but make sure I make all the decisions concerning my daughter from now on. Mr. Youngblood, don't get yourself too attached. I don't see this being a long-term situation and there's no need for either of you to get hurt."

"Don't you worry about me. I've just never had a child take such a shine to me before, and I wouldn't want to be rude toward her. Her first experience around a man shouldn't be bad."

Flannery had no idea on how to respond to that. She felt a little cornered by the statement. "Let's go eat," she said. She scooped up Savannah and headed toward the door.

When they entered the house, Jenny was slapping boiled pork onto thick slices of bread. Flannery fetched the plates as Jenny brought the platter of sandwiches and a bowl of baked beans to the table.

Jenny continued her silence during the meal until she learned of the plan for Savannah to go with Boone and Flannery on horseback. "I've never heard tell of such a foolish idea. Our little one can just stay here with me. No need to chance harm coming her way," she warned.

Flannery reached over and patted Jenny's hand. "We can't hide her away forever. She'll be fine. Just trust me."

"It's not you I'm worried about. A man that don't own no horse might not be able to even ride one. In fact, he might not be who he says he is for that matter."

Boone rubbed his forehead as he tried to decide what tact to take. He decided to be conciliatory. "I promise you that I'm Boone Youngblood, and there are two things a Texas Ranger has to be good at – one is shooting a gun and the other is riding a horse. A ranger won't survive any other way. I can assure that the last thing in the world that I want is to bring harm to that sweet child. She'll be safe."

"I might as well shut up. Seems nobody wants to listen to a wise old black woman today anyhow, but you better know I'll shoot you dead if something happens to my baby."

"Jenny, let's just eat and try to relax a little," Flannery coaxed.

The rest of the meal went without incident. As Jenny gathered up the dishes, Flannery took Savannah to change their clothes. Boone decided to walk into the den to avoid being alone with Jenny. As he began looking at the photographs on the fireplace mantel, Flannery and Savannah entered the room.

"Hell, that's me . . . Pardon my language. I'm in this picture of the Texas Rangers. That's me standing next to Jimmy. I lost my copy of this," Boone said.

Flannery walked over and pulled down the photograph. "I didn't think about this. I remember Jimmy pointing you and some of the others out now. You are the only one he ever said much about. Yes, that is definitely you. You and Jimmy look so young."

"Jimmy was young. I was just a baby," Boone said and laughed. He glanced at Flannery. She wore riding clothes, and if she had looked skinny in a dress, she looked emaciated in pants. The woman had no shape whatsoever.

"Jenny, get in here. Boone is in this photograph with Jimmy. You can put your mind to ease," Flannery called out.

Jenny walked into the room and pulled the picture out of Flannery's hand. She studied it for a moment before carefully placing it back on the mantel. "If Jimmy saw fit for you to stand next to him, maybe you are all right after all." She turned and headed back to the kitchen without saying another word.

"That's as close as you'll ever get to an apology," Flannery said and laughed.

"I'll take it. Let's go get those horses saddled."

Boone saddled up two geldings while Flannery held Savannah. When he finished, he climbed into the saddle and she passed the child up to him.

Savannah's eyes got big and she giggled. "I'm tall," she said.

"Yes, you are," Flannery said as she mounted the horse. "Let's go see what we can find."

Flannery showed Boone around the ranch, pointing out landmarks and boundaries as they rode. Savannah's constant jabbering made it hard sometimes to get a word in edgewise. When they came upon the cattle herd, they stopped to look it over.

"Looks like you've been able to maintain the herd," Boone said.

"They've been on their own for the most part. I've let things slide around here about as long as it's possible.

It's time to do some culling, and the calves need branding. We've just been getting by, to be honest."

"Do you have the money so I could get a couple of men to help with the branding for a few days?"

"I do. Do you know much about cattle?"

"I worked for a couple of ranchers after I left the Rangers until I decided life as a gambler was an easier way to make a living. I guess I've come full circle."

"I just hope you being here doesn't cause problems. I wouldn't want to be responsible for your harm."

"You wouldn't be because I'm staying of my own accord. Don't you worry yourself, though. I know how to take care of myself and I'll be on my guard. They won't surprise us twice."

"Let's go fast," Savannah said and giggled.

"You can't tell Jenny," Boone said and nudged the horse into an easy lope before Flannery had a chance to protest. Her only option was to stay close at hand.

Chapter 4

Two days after murdering Simon Cruft, Joseph figured the time had come to go pay the banker, Oscar Hamilton, a visit. He and Hunter headed to town after lunch, making their first stop at the Cattleman's Saloon. The place buzzed with news of the rancher's death. The crime seemed to be the only thing the drinkers wanted to talk about as they speculated on the culprits. Joseph and Hunter joined in on the conversations, offering their own suspects, before finishing their beers and walking to the bank.

From Oscar Hamilton's seat in his office, he spied Joseph and Hunter entering the bank. The rotund banker shot out of his chair with considerable effort and rushed into the lobby to greet the men.

"Joseph, Hunter, so good to see you. It's been awhile since you paid us a visit," Oscar said. He pumped Joseph's hand as if he was meeting a dignitary.

"We've had a busy spring," Joseph said. "Can we talk in private?"

"Most certainly. Come on into my office."

Oscar led the men into the room and shut the door. After they were seated, he offered them cigars from his humidor before choosing one for himself and taking his seat. No one spoke while the men busied themselves with biting the heads off the cigars and lighting the sticks. As they all puffed away to get the smokes burning well, a cloud of smoke hovered above them.

"So what can I do for you, Joseph?" Oscar asked.

"I'm sure you've heard about Simon's murder. It's a terrible tragedy, but nonetheless, I don't plan to let the grass grow under my feet. I figure his place will be coming up for auction soon and I want assurance that I have the credit to make the purchase."

The banker took a puff on his cigar and leaned back into his leather chair, trying to hide his dismay that the Thurgood family would already be plotting to buy the Cruft land before the body was barely cold. He stroked his mustache as he studied the men for a moment. "I see," he said. "You know you're in good standing with the bank. I don't see why there would be any problem with you buying the Cruft place as long as it didn't go for some outlandish price."

Joseph made a sly smile. "Well, Oscar, I believe you can help ensure that the land doesn't go for too much."

"Oh, how so?"

"As I'm sure you know, Wendell Starr is buying Anderson Clark's place. I assume your bank is extending the credit for that. I think he has all the land he needs for a while. You just need to tell him that he's extended his credit as far as it will go. He'll have to sit out on the bidding for the Cruft ranch."

The rancher's suggestion instantly incensed the banker. "Wendell's and this bank's business dealing are no concern to you – or any of your business, for that matter. I'm not in the habit of favoring one of our clients over another. I won't do such a thing."

"Now don't go getting yourself all riled up. I wasn't only thinking of myself. There would be a sweet reward in this for you, too. Five hundred extra dollars can buy a lot of nice things that I'm sure your wife would just love to have. You could even take yourself a nice trip to

San Francisco for that kind of money. Just think about it," Joseph said in a voice dripping with sincerity.

Oscar Hamilton's face turned bright red and his lips puckered up as if he'd bitten into a lime. "Get out of here this instant before I refuse to ever do business with you again. I will not be bought off like some cheap whore. A man is only as good as his reputation and I won't have mine sullied by the likes of you. I always knew you could be ruthless, but I never thought you'd sink to the level of a snake in the grass. You need to leave before I go get the sheriff. You make yourself highly suspect in the death of Simon if you ask me."

Joseph jumped up out of his seat and marched out of the office with Hunter in quick pursuit. They mounted up without saying a word and put their horses into a gallop on their way out of town. Once they had ridden past the last house in Trinidad, Joseph slowed his gelding to a walk.

Hunter slowed his mount to fall in beside his father. "That certainly didn't go well," he said.

"That's for sure. I thought Oscar would jump at the offer. Whoever heard of a banker with any sort of ethics? Sometimes it's hard to judge a man," Joseph said, bewilderment in his voice.

"What do we do now?"

"I guess we'll just have to see how badly Wendell wants the Cruft place. I don't think anybody else will have the means to buy it besides him and us. Let's get home and get to work."

As Joseph and Hunter traveled up their ranch road, they spotted Sheriff Stout and his deputy, Kenneth Lyons, talking to Logan and Elliot out by the barn.

Joseph had been expecting the lawmen's arrival, but the sight of them made him uneasy all the same, especially since they'd been talking to his sons without him there. Elliot was capable of saying most anything if left to his own devices. "You just keep your mouth shut and let me do all the talking," he said to Hunter.

The sheriff walked up to Joseph's horse before the rancher could dismount. "You're just the man I'm looking for," Sheriff Stout said.

"I suppose you're here because of Simon's murder. I couldn't believe it when I heard the news," Joseph said as he climbed off his horse.

"Did you do it?"

Joseph let out a sigh and cocked his head as he eyed the sheriff with a disgusted look. "No, I didn't. I considered Simon a friend and I'm right upset about the whole thing. And his killing makes me nervous. I've told all my men to stay on their toes."

"I've talked to your sons and ranch hands, and nobody seems to have seen anything out of the ordinary. What about you?"

"Not a thing."

"Some of Simon's ranch hands were branding on the day of the murder. A couple of them saw three riders off in the distance. I would assume they were the culprits. Their tracks led back this direction until they disappeared into the river. We couldn't ever find where they came out for all the cattle tracks."

"I wish I could be of some help. I truly do."

"You know, Joseph, I'll go wherever the evidence leads and I don't care who it points to. Your last name won't make a hill of beans' difference if you are a murderer."

"Sheriff, I resent such talk. My family helped make this place what it is today. We've opened our purses when the town has needed money, too. You have no call to make such insinuations without a shred of evidence."

"The whole thing seems mighty peculiar to me. Just remember that money is useless when you're swinging at the end of a rope. I'm done here for now," the sheriff said. He made a nod of his head at his deputy to signal they were leaving.

As the sheriff and deputy rode away, Joseph kicked at the ground. "If this day don't beat all. Oscar doesn't want to do us any favors at the bank and the sheriff all but pronounced me guilty. I think some people have forgotten what the Thurgood name means around these here parts. Hell, I helped get the sheriff elected. That took a lot of nerve on his part. I have a notion to make an example out of him so that people know not to mess with us."

Logan shouted out an oath. "I told you not to bother Simon, but nobody ever listens to me. You're liable to bring down our family over this. Why can't you see that this isn't the old days where you could just do whatever you saw fit? The sheriff is going to be watching us."

"Watch your mouth, boy," Joseph warned as he stepped toward his son so that their faces were inches apart. "We're the only four that know what really happened. As long as we all keep our mouths shut, the sheriff will have no cause to go arrest us. There is no evidence. Simon's ranch hands weren't close enough to identify us. I'm just looking out for my family."

"It'll serve you right if Wendell gets the Cruft place. Nothing good comes from evil intentions."

"Sometimes you are a disgrace to your name," Joseph yelled. "Get to work before I do something I'll regret."

Logan turned and stormed off toward his horse, leaving his family to watch him jump onto his mount and ride away at a gallop.

Chapter 5

When Wendell Starr's son-in-law, Calvin Broach, brought him the news of Simon Cruft's murder, Wendell shook his head and made a smug expression. "That has the handprints of Joseph Thurgood all over it," he said. "I knew Joseph would be riled up when he heard I'd bought out Anderson Clark. Never thought he'd resort to killing, though. I can't fart without Joseph having to come smell it."

Wendell was about fifteen years older than Joseph and had always been contemptuous of the younger rancher. They'd managed to coexist through the years, but the competition to expand their empires had led to tensions and distrust.

"That's what I thought, too," Calvin said.

Wendell's son, Austin, stood with them, but he was staring off into the distance as if he was in his own little world. Austin hadn't been right since he came back from the war. His doctor diagnosed him with a condition called soldier's heart, but most people just said he was touched in the head. For the most part, Austin managed to function around the ranch successfully as long as he stayed out of the liquor. Wendell tended to give him jobs where he worked alone, so that if he got frustrated, no one would be in harm's way from his violent temper. He'd broken a ranch hand's arm one time after he'd gotten startled when a horse kicked a stall wall.

"Austin, did you hear anything we said?" Wendell asked.

Austin turned his head to look at his father and brother-in-law. "Sure, I heard you. That Englishman sure talked funny, didn't he? I'll miss hearing his voice," he said before resuming his gazing toward the west.

With Austin's limited capacity to function in society, Calvin had become Wendell's right-hand man and trusted confidante. The old man made sure that his son-in-law was aware of all the goings-on concerning the ranch.

"Are we going to try to buy Cruft's ranch?" Calvin asked.

"I'll have to talk to the bank and see what they say. We did get Anderson's place cheap enough that they might extend us further. Wouldn't that be something if we bought that out from under Joseph's nose?"

"Yes, it would. It would serve them right."

"Did you hear whether the sheriff suspects them?"

"I didn't find out anything about that. Everybody was just talking about how grizzly the murders were and how Simon had to know the persons who did it. They were shot pointblank."

"We're done here for the day. Let's go pay Joseph a visit. If we're lucky, we might catch them around the house. I want to get under his skin a little. He needs to know that we're not all fools," Wendell said.

"Sounds good to me."

Wendell took Austin by the arm. "Come on. You're coming with us," he said.

The Thurgood ranch sat a good distance from Wendell's spread and took nearly an hour of travel to reach at a road trot. By the time they arrived at the road leading to Joseph's house, the time was nearing six in the evening.

"We should get there just as they're wrapping up their day," Wendell said.

"You know, we're going to be way outnumbered if there's trouble and his ranch hands are standing around. Maybe we should have brought some of our own men with us," Calvin said.

"We'll be fine. Joseph isn't a fool."

Joseph, his sons, and their ranch hands were busy unsaddling horses and putting them in the barn as the men rode up. The unexpected visitors caused a lull in the activities as everyone paused, surprised at Wendell's arrival.

"Wendell, what brings you out this way?" Joseph asked.

"We were checking on some of our cattle out this way and thought we'd just stop in for a visit," Wendell lied.

"Well, climb down and catch me up on the news. We haven't crossed paths in a good while."

Wendell swung his body out of the saddle and shook hands with Joseph. Calvin and Austin also dismounted and mingled with Joseph's sons.

Austin was keenly perceptive of other people's emotions, and as the families made small talk, the tension in the air caused him to start scratching his face so hard that he left red marks on his cheeks. Even though Logan was a good deal younger than Austin, he'd always had a soft spot for the war veteran, much the same as he did toward children. With the knowledge that Austin liked to talk about horses, Logan began a conversation with him about his horse. Austin became animated and relaxed a little as he expounded on the virtues of his mount.

Joseph knew Wendell Starr well enough to know that this visit wasn't a social call. Wendell always had an ulterior motive for whatever he did. All of their polite conversation about the merits of different breeds of bulls was just a waste of time as far as Joseph was concerned. He was ready to get down to brass tacks. "I hear you finally scared Anderson Clark into selling his place to you."

The bold proclamation gave Wendell pause. He stared at Joseph a moment and then smiled slowly. "That I did, but I didn't threaten his life, and I didn't kill him like you did Simon."

"How dare you accuse me of such a thing! You have no evidence to make such a outrageous claim."

"Me and you are the two big dogs around these here parts. You can't stand it when I one-up you. It isn't a coincidence that Simon died days after word got out that I bought Anderson's spread. You've crossed a line this time."

Joseph's sons and Calvin all started nervously eyeing each other. Austin looked as if his head worked on a swivel as he looked from one person to the next as he resumed scratching his face.

"Everybody needs to just calm down," Logan warned.

"Logan, just shut up," Joseph said.

"You best listen to your son," Wendell said. "He's the only one of you with any sense anyway. You can't just kill us like you did Simon. We might all die, but by God, we'd take a Thurgood or two with us. Use your head."

"I won't stand for such accusations," Joseph yelled and reached for his revolver.

Wendell drew his pistol. A moment later, the sound of creaking leather and clicking hammers filled the air as everyone besides Logan brandished their weapons.

Austin swung his revolver around wildly. "Pa, what do I do?" he cried out.

"Don't do anything yet. Just stay calm," Wendell said.

"You're not so cocky now, are you?" Joseph taunted. "We can kill every one of you."

"Joseph, while that may be true, you will surely die with me, as well as a son or two of yours. Are you ready to die?"

Logan stepped between his father and Wendell. "Everyone needs to put their guns away. No one will win this battle."

Austin spun so that he faced Joseph and aimed his pistol at the rancher. "I know you all think I'm crazy, but I still know how to kill. God knows I did enough of it in the war. Dying would just put me out of my misery. Either put your gun away or I'm going to kill you."

The threat actually gave Joseph a chill and he stiffened his muscles to avoid shivering. The only things he was sure of was that Austin was touched in the head and capable of most anything. He looked toward Austin, wondering how to save face.

Wendell silently cursed himself for causing the standoff. His chest felt so tight that he had a hard time inhaling air into his lungs and his gun trembled slightly. In his wildest dreams, he would have never imagined Joseph Thurgood would be foolish enough to put them all in such a situation. He realized that Austin would either kill or be killed if he didn't act quickly. "All right, I'm putting my gun away. Joseph, please do the same. We don't need to lose our sons over this." He slowly holstered his revolver.

Logan moved so that he stood in between his father and Austin. "Just stay calm, Austin. Pa is going to put his gun away right now," he said.

For the briefest of moments, Joseph considered killing Wendell. The fear of losing a son kept him from acting on his impulse. Sweat beaded up on his forehead, and he wondered if he looked weak, but the truth of the matter was that he'd acted irrationally and had endangered everyone. He returned his gun to its holster. "Boys, put your guns away. That's an order."

The ranch hands and Joseph's sons holstered their weapons. Calvin did the same. While Austin looked around at the other men, he kept his gun pointed at Logan.

"Son, put your gun away, too," Wendell encouraged.

Austin made a nod of his head and holstered his revolver.

Wendell turned toward his horse and paused as he put his hand on the saddle horn. "Logan, I'm counting on you to keep us from getting shot in the back," he said before mounting his horse.

"You'll be safe," Logan responded.

Without another word being said, the three men rode away as the others watched on.

When the Starr crew disappeared from sight, Logan turned toward his father. "You always taught us not to draw a gun unless we planned on using it. What the hell was that? You could have gotten us all killed."

Joseph started to defend himself, but stumbled badly on his words. In frustration, he shoved Logan out of his way and stomped off toward the house. "I run things around here. I don't have to justify my actions to you or anyone else," he yelled over his shoulder.

Logan threw his hands in the air and turned to watch as Wendell and others went around a bend and disappeared totally from view. "I'm going home," he said.

Wendell pulled his horse to a stop as soon as he knew that they were out of sight. "I'm sorry I got you boys into the middle of all that. I misjudged Joseph badly this time. Maybe a guilty conscience makes a man irrational. I just don't know," he said.

"Do you think we're at war with them?" Calvin asked.

"I sure hope not. Joseph should know better. Nobody wins in those situations."

Austin reached into his saddlebag and pulled out a whiskey bottle. He uncorked it and went to take a drink, but his hand shook so badly that he poured the liquor down the front of his shirt before he found his mouth. After a long gulp, he swiped the back of his hand across his face and said, "Maybe I should have gone ahead and shot Joseph. We all could've put each other out of our miseries."

Chapter 6

After three days of sunup to sundown work, Boone, a couple of town drunks, and Flannery had managed to brand all of the new calves. Boone had proven to be a no-nonsense taskmaster, managing to keep Kile and Wally sober the whole time and making them earn their pay. They had stayed with him in the bunkhouse each night and were allowed one drink in the evening after Jenny brought them their suppers.

Flannery had showed her mettle during the long days. While she had spent most of her time keeping the fire blazing, she hadn't been afraid to get her hands dirty when necessary, even going so far as trying to tackle an escaping calf and coming out on the losing end of the collision. During the many hours of branding that Boone spent with Flannery, she had occasionally flashed glimpses of the lively personality that Jimmy had always bragged about, but for the most part, she had been stoic and quiet like a person that had had the life kicked out of her. Boone thought that most of the time she seemed more like a shadow than a living, breathing person.

The morning after completing the branding, Kile and Wally made a hasty departure after Flannery paid them their wages. While both men had done honest work, they both seemed eager to resume their lives in the saloons of Trinidad.

Flannery and Boone were standing outside the house, talking about what they next needed to do on the ranch, when Jenny walked out onto the porch with

Savannah in her arms. Jenny stood there staring at them until they finally stopped talking and looked up at her.

"What is it?" Flannery asked with just a touch of annoyance in her voice.

"Now that I've gotten used to taking food to the bunkhouse again, I was going to let Boone know that it's no trouble keeping it up so he don't have to bother coming to the house all the time," Jenny answered, hiding her true intentions in a warm southern drawl.

Flannery absentmindedly nodded her head as she contemplated Jenny's words. Truth be told, she would prefer Boone take his meals in the bunkhouse, too. Jenny had provided the perfect opportunity to make it so. Boone was their hired man after all, and she didn't want Savannah to get too attached to him. Flannery was on the verge of agreeing with Jenny when a memory came to her of Jimmy bragging of Boone's decency. That thought was followed by imagining what her proper southern mother would say to such rudeness. "Boone will just have to walk to the house if he wants fed. Your old legs don't need to be doing all that extra walking," she said.

"You're the boss," Jenny said and stomped back into the house, leaving Savannah.

Boone pulled his hat from his head and ran his hand through his hair. "I can take my meals in the bunkhouse. I don't expect to be treated like family," he said.

"Nonsense. This ranch life is lonely enough without having to take your meals alone, and you were Jimmy's friend, after all. I don't think he would have had you eating alone if he were still here. Be patient with Jenny. I still think you two will end up being buddies."

Nodding his head, Boone had his doubts that he would ever be on very good terms with either Jenny or Flannery. Both women seemed to have walls built up around them that would take a cannonball to knock down. Savannah appeared to be the only one that took a shine to him. "I know I'm right charming, but I think it would fall into the miracle category to win Jenny over," he joked.

Savannah stood at the edge of the porch with her arms in the air and looking at Boone.

"Boone, take me ride," Savannah said.

Boone grinned and rubbed the hollow of his cheek. "The boss will have to make that decision, but I am going to go saddle the horses so that we can go scout out some fresh pasture. It wouldn't take much time out of our day."

Savannah turned her attention toward her mother with a smile that made Flannery ache for Jimmy. Flannery couldn't fathom how a child that had never met her father could have his exact smile. Savannah remained the only thing in life that brought her joy and made her still feel alive. She wondered if she would ruin the child by overindulging her, but she'd be damned if she would steal a little fun from her. "You can give her a little ride, but I'm telling you right now that if you ruin my daughter, I'm moving her to the bunkhouse with you," she said, sounding as if she opposed the whole idea. She picked Savannah up and started toward the house. "Let's get the jelly washed off your face. Jenny needs to worry more about keeping you clean than where people are going to eat their next meal."

Boone walked to the barn to saddle the horses while Flannery went into the house to wash Savannah's face and hands. As soon as Flannery walked through the door, she and Jenny got into a big argument about Boone taking his meals with the family and Savannah riding on a horse with him.

"Somebody's coming," Jenny said when she happened to glance out the window.

Flannery walked over and looked out the window. Her cautious nature made her alarmed to have a visitor coming. "You keep Savannah in here with you and don't come outside no matter what happens," she said. She grabbed the shotgun and darted out of the house.

Hunter Thurgood had slipped away from the ranch without telling anyone where he was going. The killing of Simon Cruft and the encounter with Wendell Starr had put him in a frenzy to acquire more land. He worried his old man might have lost his nerve after the confrontation with Wendell, and figured a good scare would be all that it took to send the widow packing. Flannery met him before he could even climb down from his horse.

"Mr. Thurgood, what brings you out this way?" Flannery asked.

"I was just out this way and thought I would pay a visit," Hunter replied as he climbed down from his gelding.

Flannery studied Hunter, trying to figure out his motive for the visit. The one thing she was sure of was that this wasn't a social visit. The Thurgood clan wasn't known for their hospitality, especially Hunter and his old man. "Mr. Thurgood, I have a ranch to run. What do you really want?"

With a menacing smile, Hunter said, "I like a woman that doesn't beat around the bush. Did you hear that

Anderson Clark is selling his spread to Wendell and that Simon Cruft was murdered?"

As Flannery tried not to show her shock at the news, she stood there stiffly without changing her wary expression. "No, I had not, but I don't see what any of that has to do with me."

"I just thought that now may be a good time for you to sell, too. Seems like things might be getting rough around these here parts."

Bristling at the comment, Flannery said, "I have no intentions of selling and I don't appreciate you coming over here suggesting such a thing. Just let me know when your family is ready to sell. I just might buy you out."

"Lady, you're barely keeping this place going. It's just a matter of time before you sell. My cattle will be shitting all over your husband's grave over there before long." With a smirk, Hunter pointed toward Jimmy's grave.

Boone walked out of the barn, leading the saddled geldings. He caught sight of Flannery talking to a stranger. Their rigid postures informed him that the conversation was not of a pleasant nature. He picked up his pace and hustled over to stand by Flannery's side.

Hunter eyed the unexpected intruder with a leer. "Who are you?" he asked, disdain dripping from his voice.

"Where I come from, it's not considered polite to ask a stranger's name without first introducing yourself." Boone smiled as if he just might be the most congenial man in Trinidad.

"I'm guessing you came from a back room of a cathouse. You probably don't even know your daddy or have a last name. In fact, you look like a half-breed to me. I bet you've got some Injun in you. Now what's your name, boy?"

Boone rested his hand on his revolver. "I'll tell you who I am. I'm the man that's warning you that you better leave right now unless you want to see which one of us is about to die, and I'll guarantee you that that will be you."

Hunter let out a snicker. "You have no idea who you're dealing with. We'll settle this at another time, but I promise you that you'll come to rue this day." He turned to mount his horse.

"That's what I thought – all bark and no bite. You're just a coward."

Hunter spun toward Boone, but the former Ranger stood ready. Boone punched Hunter in the mouth. The blow staggered him, and before he could recover, Boone caught him with a left hook that dropped the rancher to the ground. Boone pulled out his revolver and trained it on the prone man.

"You better get out of here with whatever shred of dignity you still own," Boone warned.

It took Hunter a good minute to get to his feet. Blood dripped onto his shirt from his busted lips as he wobbled toward his horse. With considerable effort, he mounted his horse and rode off without uttering another word.

When Hunter had disappeared from sight, Flannery whirled toward Boone. Her face looked red, and her eyes and mouth were scrunched up in anger. "You might as well just shoot us all now. We're as good as dead. I should have known letting you stay here was a mistake. For God's sake, mind you own business. I was handling Hunter just fine." She shoved the shotgun into

Boone's hands and stalked toward one of the geldings. With strength that belied her boney appearance, she swung herself into the saddle. A moment later, she departed in a cloud of dust.

Boone stood dumbfounded as he watched Flannery ride away. He turned to grab the remaining horse to go after her when Jenny, carrying Savannah, walked out onto the porch.

"Hold it there, Boone. I've known that girl since the day she came into this world, and there ain't no reasoning with her when she's mad. She gets plume crazy when she's like that and what comes out of her mouth don't always come from her thoughtful mind. Just let her cool down."

As Boone turned to face Jenny, he threw his free arm into the air. "I suppose you're going to yell at me, too. Go ahead and get it over with. Maybe coming here was a mistake. I can put my old clothes back on and leave here the way I came," he hollered.

Jenny actually smiled at him. "I'm not mad. I heard every word that Flannery said, that you said, and that Hunter said. You did right as far as I'm concerned. Flannery don't want to upset any of the ranchers, but if they want this place, they're coming whether they're mad or not. You just served them notice that they ain't taking it without a fight. I just might have been wrong about you."

Boone let out a snort. "The day I figure out women, is the day I just might get rich. What should I do then?"

Jenny held Savannah out toward Boone. "Put that shotgun down and take our baby. You promised her a ride, and I believe you are a man of your word. You just be careful with my little Savannah. I plan to do a better job raising her than I did Flannery." She let out a belly laugh that shook her whole body.

Boone leaned the shotgun up against the porch and mounted the horse. When Jenny handed Savannah to him, the child let out a squeal.

"Go fast," Savannah said.

"Maybe when you're older," Boone said, trying his best to sound serious.

He waited until they were out of sight of the house before he put the horse into an easy lope. Savannah let out another squeal as they raced across the pasture.

Jenny sat on the porch, peeling potatoes, when Flannery returned on her lathered up horse. The old woman barely looked up, hoping that acting nonchalant would prevent Flannery from getting herself all worked up again now that she had returned.

"Where's Savannah?" Flannery asked from atop her horse.

"She's out riding with Boone," Jenny replied.

"What? How could you let her go with him?"

"It was your idea. What do you mean?"

"I never intended for them to go out alone. I planned on being close at hand. No better than you like Boone, I can't believe you did such a thing. Jenny, what were you thinking?"

Jenny set the pan of potatoes down and stood with her hands dug into her hips. "You make no sense whatsoever. If you were so worried, you should have stayed around instead of throwing your fit and riding off like a child. Boone certainly would do that child no harm."

"They could trip in a groundhog hole or God knows what. And what if Hunter comes back?" Flannery tossed her hat onto the porch and ran her hands through her hair. Her eyes started to well with tears.

"Hunter isn't coming back today, and when he does, he'll be bringing some help with him," Jenny said, trying to sound soothing in consideration of Flannery's state of mind.

"You don't know that."

"Boone put the fear into that man. I saw it. Hunter doesn't want any more of that today."

"But he could come back and ambush Boone and Savannah like someone did Jimmy."

"Maybe on another day, but not today. Right now, Hunter is licking his wounds and wondering how he's going to explain to his daddy how he got his lips all busted up. We know now to be on our toes. They won't surprise us twice."

"I fear Boone has stirred a hornet's nest. We just didn't need this."

"Flannery, if they want this land, they are going to come for it no matter what. Hunter came here today to cause trouble, and now he knows we ain't going down without a fight. We aren't quitters. If we survived a whole army trying to destroy Vicksburg, we can survive this, too. And I'll tell you one thing – I want old Boone on my side when the trouble starts."

Flannery managed to smile. "For someone that didn't want to even break bread with Boone earlier today, you sure are singing his praises now."

"Yes, I am. That man showed me a whole other side when he stood up to Hunter. I didn't see that coming. I admit that I was wrong. Those are some words you should learn how to say once in a while, too."

"Jenny, sometimes I don't know what I'm going to do with you, but I can't imagine how I'd survive without you."

"I'm going to take my potatoes inside and finish peeling them. Maybe you should wait on the porch for Boone and Savannah to return." Jenny gave Flannery a wink before disappearing inside the house.

Boone and Savannah returned a few minutes later. As Boone passed Savannah down to her mother, the little girl smiled ear to ear. For his part, Boone showed no emotion as he climbed down from the horse and tied it to the hitching post.

"Boone is fun," Savannah said.

"I'm glad you had a nice time, dear," Flannery said.

Boone turned toward Flannery. "I'll make no apology for my actions. I would do it all over again, but if you believe that me being here puts all of you in danger, I'll gladly go my own way. I can leave here the way I came. I certainly didn't intend to be a burden."

Flannery made a sympathetic smile and rubbed her chin as she worked up the courage to speak. "Jenny assures me that I was all wrong about how I handled things today, and we all know that Jenny is right about everything," Flannery said, glancing toward the window to see if they were being watched. "But I know she's right. Boone, I really do need to be the one that apologizes. I badly overreacted earlier. Please forgive me so that we can just get back to work and put this behind us if you are willing. I was wrong."

The apology caught Boone so off guard that he couldn't help but smile. "You're the boss," he said.

Chapter 7

Before Hunter returned to work on the ranch after his encounter with Boone, he headed to his home to change his bloodstained shirt. He gave his wife, Jill, a curt "Mind your own business." when she asked what had happened, and then he quickly departed. The change of attire proved pointless with his lips swelled to twice their normal size and a dark bruise forming on his jaw. His father and brothers all did double takes when he rode up to help them with the branding of calves.

"Where have you been and what in the hell happened to you?" Joseph asked his son.

"I don't want to talk about it," Hunter mumbled as he climbed down from his horse.

"What'd you say? I don't give a damn what you want. You better start talking unless you want a black eye and bloodied nose to go with those busted lips."

"I paid a visit to the Vogel ranch. The widow's got some young buck working for her that sucker punched me," Hunter replied much to his chagrin.

"Well, I hope you made him sorry for that."

Hunter glanced down at his feet and did not answer.

"Well, I'll be. This just gets better by the minute."

"Pa, I could barely get back on my horse. I've had horses kick me that weren't as hard as he punched."

"Have you ever seen this man before today?"

"No, sir. I don't know where he came from, but he's not from around here as far as I know."

Joseph took a deep breath and nodded his head. "Now, I want to know what you were doing over at the

Vogel place in the first place." His face had gotten redder with each question. He looked like a teapot ready to sing.

"I just thought that we needed to do something bold after Wendell came here. That woman is barely keeping that ranch going," Hunter answered.

"Damn it, I already decided we would just wait until she failed. Logan is right that we don't need the town turning on us. Don't do the thinking around here – you're not any good at it. Go help Elliot with the branding."

Joseph turned toward Logan after his other two sons had walked away. "I have a good notion to go over to the Vogel place and settle the score with that cowboy. We can't have people disrespecting us like that," he fumed.

"Pa, do you really think that man sucker punched Hunter? How would that even happen? I'd say Hunter picked on the wrong fellow and paid the price. He never could fight worth a darn anyway. Just let it blow over."

"We have our name to think about."

"That's right, and it doesn't need to be associated with picking on a widow with a little child."

Joseph looked away at the mountains to the northwest and studied them a moment. "You do have a point. I wonder how much longer that widow can hold on. This new man may prolong the inevitable."

"I don't know, but you'd better get it through Hunter's head to leave them alone. He's liable to sneak back over there and do something stupid if you don't."

Joseph nodded his head before strolling over to where Hunter stood hunched over while branding a calf. When Hunter finished, he straightened his posture and turned to return the brand to the fire. Joseph grabbed his son by the shirt and nearly yanked him off his feet.

With their faces nearly touching, Joseph said, "If you so much as go near the Vogel ranch again, I'll put a brand on your forehead. Do I make myself clear?"

"Sure, Pa. I'll leave them alone. I promise," Hunter stammered.

"You better not forget," Joseph said. He gave his son a hard shove. "Get to work."

∞

Boone sat at the supper table and watched Jenny, amazed at the change in her demeanor. By the way she acted, he could almost convince himself that they were lifelong friends. He still had a hard time getting his head around the fact that standing up to Hunter Thurgood had changed her opinion of him so much. Every time there was a lull in the conversation, she would entertain them with some anecdote.

Flannery waited until Jenny finally hushed. "So do you think the two of us will be able to drive the herd to the new grazing spot?" she asked.

Boone had just chomped off a big chunk of meat from a chicken thigh. He opened his mouth to speak and then thought better of it. Nobody was going to blame him for teaching Savannah bad manners. He held up a finger to buy some time as he quickly chewed the food and nearly got choked when he swallowed too soon. "I think so. If we can get that old bull to moving, the rest should follow."

"I sure hope so. The cattle have been fending for themselves for so long that they've probably forgotten what it's like to be driven."

"We'll get them," Boone said with a tone of certainty.

Savannah listened intently to the conversation. "I go," she said.

Boone looked over at the child. "No, that might be dangerous. I'll give you a ride when we get back," he said, and then realized what he had done. "Oh, I'm sorry. That wasn't my place to say."

Flannery waved her hand through the air. "No, that's fine. She might as well learn that you're not just her play toy. I don't want you more popular than me anyway."

The attempt at humor made Boone smile. He had about decided that Flannery was void of such a thing.

Jenny jumped up from the table. "You all need to quit talking and get to eating. I made us an apple pie today. It's going to get moldy at the rate you all are gabbing."

Boone and Flannery exchanged puzzled glances. Jenny had done the vast amount of the talking throughout the meal.

"What got into you?" Flannery asked. "I think the last time you baked was a birthday. I thought we must be out of lard."

"Oh, hush. It's been a while since we had something to rejoice about."

"I'm still not convinced we have anything to celebrate. There are a lot more Thurgoods than there are of us," Flannery said.

"But now they know we aren't just sitting here for the taking."

Boone, fearing an argument could erupt at any moment, looked up and smiled. "I would have punched me a cowboy on the first day I came here if I knew I would have gotten some apple pie out of the deal."

∞

Just before sundown, Wendell went for a ride just to get away by himself and think. He hadn't slept well the night before for worrying over Austin. Years ago, his son's doctor had been sure that time would heal whatever ailed Austin, but the truth of the matter was that he'd been getting progressively worse from the day he returned from the war. Austin had pretty much stayed drunk ever since the showdown with the Thurgood clan. His hands shook constantly and he sweated profusely. Sometimes his speech made no sense whatsoever. At times like this, Wendell longed to talk with his deceased wife, Elizabeth. She could always make him feel as if everything would turn out fine, and had been the one that could bring Austin back around whenever he got really out of control.

As Wendell returned to his home, he found his son-in-law, Calvin, standing there waiting for him.

"I just found Austin passed out in the barn. Do you want me to go get Kelly and see if she can talk to him?" Calvin asked.

Kelly was Wendell's daughter and Calvin's wife. She and Austin had been close before the war, but for some reason, he seemed to resent her now. When they were together, Austin would usually find a way to start an argument with his sister. Through it all, Wendell remained grateful that Calvin handled the situation so well and didn't seem to resent Austin's boorish behavior.

"Nah, I don't think it would do any good and he'd most likely just upset her. Kelly has her hands full raising those two granddaughters of mine anyway," Wendell said.

"That's for sure. I don't know what happens to girls when they get into their teens, but I hope I get my old Sally and Renee back one of these days."

Wendell made a little snorting sound. "Oh, you will, but it'll be one of these years, not days."

Calvin smiled and then turned serious. "I tried talking to Austin, but he wasn't having any of it. I don't know what else to do."

"I appreciate the effort and the fact that you tolerate Austin. You could resent him and make things difficult around here. I couldn't have ended up with a better son-in-law if I tried."

The compliment embarrassed Calvin. Wendell wasn't in the habit of handing them out, and Calvin didn't know how to respond. He stood there rigidly and nodded his head.

"Go on and get home. I'll take care of Austin," Wendell said.

Wendell waited until Calvin had ridden out of sight before walking into the barn where he found Austin stretched out in a pile of straw. He pulled the whiskey bottle out of his son's hand and took a swig. As he gazed down at Austin, he thought about the proud young man that had ridden off to war with plans to help save the Union. The man sleeping before him now looked to be just a shell of that soldier. Wendell dropped down beside Austin and waited.

By the time Austin began stirring, night had fallen. In the meantime, Wendell had lit an oil lamp and killed off the rest of the whiskey. Austin awakened with a start, kicking Wendell as he did so and startling him, too.

"You've been asleep in the barn," Wendell said, hoping to ease his son's mind.

"Where's my whiskey?" Austin asked.

"I drank it all. You need to sober up anyway. Sit up and let's talk."

Austin struggled to get into a sitting position. "What do you want to talk about?"

"What do you think? You. Austin, you can't just turn into a drunk. You need to lay off the bottle and act like a man. It's time to fight through this."

"Do you think I like my life? If I knew how to fix myself, I would." Austin covered his eyes with his hand to protect them from the light of the lamp. The glow felt like it burned through his brain.

"The war has been over for fifteen years. Why can't you just put it behind you?"

"Because it was yesterday to me. A loud noise will send me looking for cover every time. And I can still see the carnage as clearly as if I were looking at it right before me now. And good God, the smells. Do you have any idea what a battlefield smells like after bodies have been lying in the sun for three days? That atrocity is seared into my nostrils forever."

Wendell didn't speak for a moment. He tossed the empty bottle against a stall wall and looked at his son. "But what good does it do to dwell on all that?"

"You just don't understand. I don't dwell on it. It dwells on me."

Chapter 8

Boone still had a hard time believing in the transformation Jenny had gone through toward him. In the days since he had stood up to Hunter, she had treated him as one of the family without showing any signs whatsoever of any of the apprehension she had previously displayed. As the four of them ate breakfast, Jenny held court with stories about Flannery's childhood that were clearly not appreciated. Flannery would cut her eyes at Jenny and scowl, but the old black woman would just smile, undeterred by the looks she received.

When Jenny paused to take a bite of eggs, Flannery said to Boone, "Jimmy never told me anything about your past. Where did you grow up?"

"That's because Jimmy didn't know. As far as I'm concerned, I was born on the day Jimmy didn't kill me for cheating at cards. Everything before that isn't worth repeating," Boone answered.

"Oh, I see. Sometimes I'd like to pretend I didn't have a past instead of listening to Jenny tell the whole world about it."

"You shouldn't have lived it if you didn't want me telling about it," Jenny snapped.

Flannery dismissively shook her head. "Well, I'm headed to town for some supplies after we're through eating," she announced.

Jenny swallowed without chewing her food in order to speak. "You need to take Boone with you now that Hunter is all stirred up," she said.

"I will do no such thing. I've been going to Trinidad alone since we moved here, and I continued after Jimmy's murder. I see no reason to stop now."

The truth of the matter was that Flannery would have felt a lot safer with Boone accompanying her, but she didn't want anyone to perceive her as weak or scared. She also didn't want the rumors to start that she now had a man in her life. The old ladies of Trinidad would be in a lather talking about her if she came to town with Boone.

"You're just being plain old hardheaded now. That little girl right there needs a mother. She's already lost enough."

"I'm quite aware of what Savannah has lost. I don't think Hunter or anyone else is going to do me harm. The subject is closed."

Boone continued eating as he watched the two women bickering. He had no intention of getting involved in the quarrel. From what he could tell, Flannery was too headstrong to be swayed in letting him come along with her anyway. She'd only get mad at him, too, and he would just as soon stay on her good side, be that what it may. He found Flannery to be quite the confusing woman. Sometimes, she would drop her guard and let her personality come through with him, but most times, he felt as if she kept him away with a ten-foot pole.

"I've known you long enough to know there's no changing your mind. You was a stubborn child and you're still stubborn," Jenny said. She grabbed her biscuit and took a big bite.

After they finished eating breakfast, Boone helped Flannery hitch the horses to the buckboard. She wasted no time in grabbing her shotgun and heading toward town. Boone and Jenny stood in the yard and watched Flannery ride out of sight as Savannah played at their feet.

Jenny put her hands on her hips. "If Hunter shoots her, maybe it'll be in the head. Most likely, a bullet would just bounce off the thick skull that girl has."

Boone smiled. "You and her sure have an interesting relationship," he said.

"You mean cause I'm a black woman sassing a white woman?"

The question gave Boone pause for a moment as he hesitated in answering her. "Yeah, I guess so."

"I weren't no slave, and I got paid a fair wage. I was part of the family. Mr. and Mrs. Simpson treated me like I was an aunt that lived with them. They celebrated my birthday and gave me gifts just like everybody else. I was a second momma to Flannery and the other children," Jenny said with pride welling up in her voice.

"Didn't you ever want to have a husband and your own family?"

"Sure, I did, but let me tell you, the pickings were slim when it came to free black men, and I wasn't about to marry me no slave. Flannery and the other children were just like my own anyway. I've had me a good life with the Simpsons."

"I'm glad to hear that. Everybody deserves to be happy. Flannery sure seems different than the person Jimmy used to wax on about around the campfire. I guess losing your husband will do that to you."

Jenny smiled as she thought back to Flannery's childhood. "Before the war, she was the liveliest child I did ever see in my life. My, she could be sassy and hardheaded. I've spanked that girl's behind more times than I can count. Never did no good though," she said and laughed. "Mr. Simpson worked as a cotton trader, and we lived in a big fancy house until the siege of Vicksburg. We was forced to live in a cave carved out of the side of a hill. We all got sick with cholera. Flannery's little sister, Josie, died from it. Flannery was never the same after that. I think she always felt guilty that she lived and her sister didn't."

"That's a sad story. That war was a terrible thing. I sure don't regret being too young to fight in it. Jimmy sure had some tales from those days."

"It was a sad time, but life goes on. After the war, Mr. Simpson got his business going again and repaired the house. We went back to living the good life."

Boone nodded his head, lost in thought. "I guess Jimmy helped Flannery get past all that," he mused.

"That's an interesting topic. I'm not sure if he helped her put the past behind her or if she just kept the darkness from him. Don't get me wrong, she'd found happiness, but sometimes when it was just me and her, I could still see Josie's death weighing on her. Of course, now that Jimmy's gone, she's worse than ever. She's been through a lot for one so young. Thank goodness, she has Savannah. I'd give anything to have my old Flannery back."

"Jenny, you're a good friend to Flannery."

Jenny grinned. "Yes, I am. I'd have to be to put up with all the grief that woman gives me. We'd better get to work or she'll be giving it to both of us. And don't you dare say a word to her about any of this. If she knew what I've told you, she'd be raising the roof tonight."

"Don't you worry about that. I'm real good with keeping secrets."

Jenny scooped up Savannah and headed for the house to do some chores while Boone went to the barn to repair some tack he'd noticed needed tending.

Flannery returned home a little before noon, just in time to join the others for lunch. After eating, they unloaded the supplies from the wagon, and then she and Boone got to work on cleaning the barn.

When they finished their task in the midafternoon, both were sweaty and stinky. Flannery wiped her brow with her sleeve and then reached into her pocket to produce some gold coins. "I paid a visit to the bank today. I thought maybe you would like some wages," she said.

Boone smiled. "Why, yes I would. I've been planning on buying me a new hat when I got paid. Jimmy's head was a little bigger than mine and this one keeps slipping down my forehead."

"We've got a lot done since you've been here. Why don't you get cleaned up and head to town then."

"Thank you, ma'am. I believe I'll do that."

"Boone, you can call me Flannery. In fact, I insist on it. You were Jimmy's friend, after all."

"Well, Flannery, I'll just do that then, too," Boone said. He smiled as he bounced the coins in his hand.

"I don't suppose you'll be home until after dark. I probably won't see you until morning. Be careful," Flannery said before walking out of the barn.

Boone hustled to the bunkhouse to retrieve a clean change of clothes and a bar of soap before heading to the creek. After giving himself a good scrubbing, he wasted no time in setting out for town on the gelding he always rode.

Trinidad caught Boone by surprise. The town looked much bigger and bustling than he had imagined, with a main street lined with businesses and saloons. He rode down the street until he found a hatmaker's shop and went inside the establishment. The shopkeeper had a wide array of hats to choose from to the point that Boone had a hard time making a decision. With the storeowner growing impatient, Boone chose a brown Stetson.

Boone's next stop was the first saloon he came upon. He walked into the Cattleman's Saloon and ordered a beer. The place looked cleaner and better lit than most drinking establishments with a clientele of cowboys and businessmen. It seemed as if it had been forever since he'd had a beer and he savored each sip as he eyed his surroundings. A poker game was going on in the back of the room and he resisted the urge to go check it out. He didn't have enough wages for a good stake to play anyway.

Just as Boone struck up a conversation with a cowboy standing next to him at the bar, he caught sight of three men entering the saloon. The man leading the way was Hunter Thurgood. Boone swore under his breath. One of the other men was obviously a brother to Hunter based on their resemblance. The third man was tall and lanky, and didn't look hard and ornery like the brothers.

"Well, look here. If it isn't Flannery Vogel's new bed warmer," Hunter hollered out.

The pronouncement caused the saloon to go quiet as everyone turned their heads to look at Hunter.

Boone spun to face his nemesis. "You probably shouldn't go running your mouth at me until your lips heal from the last whipping I gave you," he warned.

"You sucker punched me."

"So, not only are you a bully, but you're a liar, too. You spun to draw down on me and I was ready for you. Sucker punching and being prepared for battle are not the same things."

Logan reached over and put his hand on Hunter's shoulder. "Pa said to leave the widow alone. Just let it go," he said.

"I am leaving the widow alone. Just stay out of this, Logan. Pa didn't say anything about me crossing paths with the likes of him."

The saloon owner made a slight nod of his head at one of his bouncers. The man made a quick exit out the saloon entrance.

Boone glanced over at Logan, surprised that he was a brother to Hunter. Logan certainly looked to be the pick of the litter, and appeared as if he might have some intelligence about him. The notion came to Boone that maybe he could reason with him. "I really don't want any trouble. As long as your family leaves Flannery and us alone, we'll be good."

Hunter let out a derisive laugh. "Did you hear that? *Flannery*. I bet you have all kinds of names for the widow when you have her under the covers."

Logan grabbed Hunter by the arm and attempted to drag him away, but Hunter took his free hand and shoved his brother, nearly causing him to fall across a table.

"I don't care what you say or think about me, but you best watch your mouth when it comes to the widow," Boone said as he rested his hand on his revolver.

Sheriff Stout and Deputy Lyons came barreling into the saloon with their guns drawn.

"What's going on here?" the sheriff called out.

"Hunter is making trouble with this lad," the saloonkeeper replied.

"Both of you get your hands away from your guns," Sheriff Stout ordered. "Now who are you?"

Boone raised his hands chest high. "I'm Boone Youngblood. I'm helping Flannery Vogel on her ranch. Her husband, Jimmy, and I were Texas Rangers together."

The news caused the sheriff to raise his eyebrows in surprise, and his shoulders relaxed a little. "And what problem do you have with Hunter?"

"He paid the widow a visit a few days ago and tried to bully her into selling out to him. We exchanged pleasantries."

The sheriff let out a little laugh. "I bet you did."

"Don't I get to tell my side of the story?" Hunter asked.

"You just shut up until you're spoken to," the sheriff said.

"That figures."

Sheriff Stout turned his attention back to Boone. "Jimmy was a good man. I'm sorry for your loss and that I could never find his killer, though I wouldn't be surprised if he wasn't standing right in front of you. I bet you and Jimmy had some wild times as Rangers."

"Yes, sir, we did. We always had each other's back through thick and thin. I owe everything to that man."

The sheriff nodded his head before looking toward Hunter. "You and your old man are about to get on my last nerve. You'd best leave the widow alone if you don't want to deal with me. And besides, Boone is liable to kill you. Looks like he's already splattered your lips."

"Why are you taking the word of some drifter? He could be making up the whole story," Hunter protested.

"I doubt that. Just like I told your pa, I don't care how much money you have if you're guilty of a crime. You'll end up in my jail if you're not careful. You'll slip up one of these days and that will be the end of it. You need to watch yourself."

"My pa helped get you elected. You best watch yourself."

"Logan, get your brother out of here before I crack his head open."

"Come on, Hunter," Logan said.

"But this is where we drink."

"Not today," Sheriff Stout said.

Logan and Elliot each grabbed one of their brother's arms and started leading him out of the saloon.

The sheriff walked up beside Boone. "Jeb, get this man another beer. We have some talking to do."

Chapter 9

The morning after Boone's encounter with Hunter in the saloon, Flannery's face drained of color as she sat at the breakfast table listening to him tell of his adventure. She covered her mouth with her hand and slowly shook her head as she gazed at Boone.

"I knew he wouldn't let it go. He's a lot like his daddy," Flannery said.

"I didn't start it, but I wasn't about to back down either," Boone said.

"At least you won over Sheriff Stout. That's something."

"The tall brother, I think his name was Logan, seemed to be a much more reasonable fellow."

"Yes, I believe he is, but he doesn't have much say from what I hear. Joseph and Hunter are the two that we have to worry about. Elliot, the youngest one, just goes along with whatever the old man wants."

Jenny clasped her hands together and peered at Boone and then toward Flannery. "There's no call to get all worked up over this. Having the sheriff being friendly to us should make the Thurgoods think twice before they try something else. We're going to be fine. I can just feel it. Our luck is changing," she said.

Flannery rolled her eyes. "Since when did you acquire such a sunny disposition? I don't see anything for which to feel overjoyed. Jenny, this is serious."

"I've been the sunny one around here for a long time. You're the girl that sees trouble around every corner.

Honestly, Flannery, you need to start counting your blessings and get on with life."

Boone, fearing an all-out war between the women, and against his better judgement, decided to intervene. "Ladies, there's no need for us to get all worked up against each other. One way or the other, we'll deal with what comes our way – good and bad. We just need to make the best of the situation."

Jenny smiled at Boone, but Flannery cut her eyes his way and gave him a look that would have put fear into a lesser man. Boone ignored the glare and smiled congenially at both the women.

With a sigh, Flannery drained the last of the coffee from her cup and stood. "We've certainly done enough talking for one morning. Let's get to work."

∞

Joseph Thurgood stood outside the barn with Logan, Elliot, and his ranch hands as they waited for Hunter to arrive at the ranch. The men all lingered there quietly, shifting their weight from one foot to the other. With the rancher's dour expression on display, the group felt afraid to talk for fear of unleashing his wrath upon them.

A few minutes later, Hunter came riding up with his horse in a lope. "Sorry I'm late. Jill needed some help this morning," he said as he climbed off his horse.

Joseph walked up to his son and backhanded him in the mouth. The unexpected blow knocked Hunter back a couple of steps before he regained his balance. His already wounded lips began spurting blood.

"I told you to leave Flannery Vogel alone," Joseph hollered.

"I have. You didn't say nothing about her ranch hand. I had to call him out when I saw him in the saloon," Hunter pleaded before wiping the blood from his chin.

"You knew damn well what I meant. The sheriff is already giving us trouble and now you have him budding up to this man that claims to have been a Texas Ranger. You don't mess with those Rangers. They have a well-deserved reputation for being a mean lot. You're lucky he didn't do more than bust your lips."

Hunter glared at Logan. "You had to run your big mouth, didn't you? You think you're so high and mighty."

Before Logan had a chance to defend himself, his father said, "Logan didn't say a word to me about it. It was Elliot, and it's a damn good thing he did. If I'd heard this from someone else, I'd really be pissed. Your brothers are just looking out for you. For God's sake, Hunter, use your head. Now let's get to work."

"I'm not a boy and I refuse to be treated like one. I've had about all the grief from you that I'm going to take. Work your own damn ranch," Hunter yelled. He turned and swung himself into the saddle.

"Boy, you aren't going anywhere. We have a ranch to run," Joseph said as he moved to grab the reins.

Hunter spun the horse around and was gone in a gallop, sending dust drifting over the men.

"Do you want me to go and try to talk some sense into him?" Logan asked.

"Nah, we'll just let him cool down some. He'll come back when he's ready. I probably should have done that in private and not embarrassed him, but I've got to get it through his head to leave them alone. We don't need any more trouble right now," Joseph said. "Let's get busy."

∞

Boone and Flannery spent the day expanding the corral. Jimmy had regretted the dimensions he'd chosen for the pen almost from the moment he'd finished the project. As Boone dug the fencepost holes, Flannery had carried the posts and boards over from a pile of lumber that Jimmy had stacked. They worked mostly in silence, but well together. She would help him set each post and tamp the dirt into the hole. By two o'clock, both of them were exhausted from their labors.

"Let's go check on the herd and make sure none of the calves are ailing from the branding. My arms are going to fall off if we do another post," Flannery said.

"You won't get any argument from me," Boone replied.

Flannery smiled. "I guess there's a first time for everything."

Boone found himself caught off guard any time Flannery flashed her sense of humor. Wittiness was something he just never expected from her. Most times the woman just didn't seem to possess any of it whatsoever.

"I like to keep you guessing."

"I don't have to guess. Now that you and Jenny are big buddies, it seems I'm always getting ganged up on around here."

"Maybe we just have better heads on our shoulders." Boone then smirked at her.

"Yes, you certainly made a marvelous first impression on me when I found you sleeping in my straw in your dapper wardrobe. I've been in awe of you ever since then."

Boone let out a cackle. "You have me there."

"I liked it better when Jenny didn't like you. I've never seen her change her opinion about someone so fast in all the time I've known her – which is forever."

"It's the Boone Youngblood charm. I just have a way with the ladies – at least most of them."

Flannery laughed with her whole body. In that moment, Boone saw for the first time, the woman that Jimmy must have fell in love with. She looked pretty and feminine. The change in demeanor was shocking and even a little arousing.

"Let's ride before you manage to ruin the moment," Flannery said. She marched off toward the horses.

They had ridden about a mile from the house and were crossing a flat close to where they had driven the herd earlier in the week when Boone thought he caught movement out of the corner of his eye, up on a side of a hill. He turned his head and peered off into the distance, unable to spot anything, but he had a foreboding that they were in danger. His years of fighting Indians had given him a healthy respect for ambushes, and he and Flannery were sitting ducks at the moment.

"Head for the creek – quick," Boone yelled.

Flannery looked stunned, and she paused a moment before spurring her horse and turning it hard left toward the creek. As they raced toward their destination, the rear of Flannery's horse collapsed a tic of a clock before the sound of the gunshot reached them. The jar from the horse hitting the ground unseated Flannery from the saddle and she smacked into the grass. She jumped to her feet and looked around as if she were trying to understand what had happened. At the sound of the shot, Boone had glanced over his shoulder and recognized what was happening. He tugged on the reins to slow his mount and then spun the animal around. Just as he was about to use his horse to shield Flannery, a second shot kicked up dirt at her feet.

"Get up here with me," Boone shouted as he kicked his foot out of the stirrup.

Still feeling a little dizzy from her fall, Flannery struggled with her balance when she lifted her foot toward the stirrup as another shot rang out from the hillside. Boone, realizing the dire situation, grabbed Flannery by the back of her blouse and slung her up behind him. His action nearly disrobed her, but she wrapped her arms around his waist and he spurred the horse into a gallop. They zigzagged their way toward the creek while the gunfire continued. As they neared the creek, Boone never even attempted to slow the horse. He jumped the animal from the bank into the creek bed and pulled it to a stop. While Flannery slid off the horse's back, Boone retrieved the rifle from the scabbard and dismounted.

"Are you hurt?" Boone asked as they took cover along the bank.

"I'm fine. I was just a little disoriented," Flannery replied. She tugged her blouse back down over her midriff. "That's the quickest I've ever had a man undress me."

The comment came so unexpectedly that Boone couldn't help but chuckle in spite of the dire circumstances. He was quickly coming to realize that he didn't know Flannery very well at all. The woman might be as unpredictable as the weather.

"Sorry about that. I wasn't in the mood to be used for target practice."

"You did what you had to do. Don't worry about it. What are we going to do now?"

Boone peeked his head up above the bank to survey the situation. A shot rang out, kicking up dust well short of its target. "Good news – bad news. We must be 150 yards away. It'll take a heck of a shot to hit us, but the same goes for me hitting him."

"Are you a good shot?"

"Flannery, I served a Texas Ranger. Jimmy proved to be a fine shot, but I was better."

"It has to be Hunter, doesn't it?"

"I would say so. Some people just don't know when to quit."

"If you kill him, I fear an all-out war. Joseph Thurgood is not someone that will let such a thing go without retribution."

"Well, we can just start walking toward Hunter. I'm sure he'll dial in his aim eventually."

Flannery frowned and cut her eyes at Boone. "I didn't suggest such a thing whatsoever. If he doesn't leave, there isn't much alternative."

Boone and Hunter began exchanging gunfire. Each time Boone fired, he'd take cover long enough for Hunter to shoot and then take slow deliberate aim before pulling the trigger again.

Flanner sat with her back to the creek bank, watching Boone. "I thought you were a good shot. Doesn't look like it to me," she said.

"I haven't even aimed at him yet."

"What?"

"I'm shooting at the rock he's hiding behind to see how much my bullet is dropping. I'm ready for business now," Boone said and winked.

"Can you try to just wound him?"

Boone rolled his eyes. "Not likely since his head is about all that ever appears. I guess I could try to shoot an ear off if you like," he said in a voice dripping with sarcasm.

"Honestly, some of the things you say. I'm not sure if you're trying to be funny or you're that full of yourself."

"Sorry. That was an attempt at humor. I guess we could hold hands and cry about our impending demise."

"See, there you go again."

"All right, no more. I'm sorry."

Flannery rested her head against the embankment. "No, I'm the one that should be sorry. I just realized that I forgot to thank you for rescuing me. You could have left me behind to save yourself or you could have gotten yourself killed when you came back for me. I truly am grateful."

"I would have left you behind if not for Savannah. I figured Jenny and I would ruin her with all the spoiling we would do on her if you weren't around to squash all the fun."

Flannery shook her head before picking up a pebble that she hurled at Boone. "You really are insufferable."

Boone didn't respond. He'd readied his Winchester and concentrated on his aim. A moment later the roar of his gun made Flannery jump even though she knew he was about to fire. After the shot, Boone sat down and leaned his back against the bank.

"I sure hope me coming here won't turn out to be the ruin of you," Boone said. "Maybe things would have blown over if I hadn't stirred Hunter up so."

"You just killed him, didn't you?"

Boone turned his head so that he looked Flannery in the eye. "He's either dead or dying."

"This didn't start with you. This started when they killed Jimmy. We're finishing this for him. I've always suspected that it was the Thurgoods anyway."

Boone nodded his head and stood. "Let's go see what I did."

They rode together to the injured horse where Boone put the animal out of its misery before traveling on to the bottom of the hill where they walked up the incline. Hunter lay sprawled on his back with a bullet hole in his right cheek. His eyes were still open and he looked as if he was staring at the sky. From all appearances, he seemed to have died instantly.

Flannery covered her mouth and looked away. Her body sagged as if she were wilting. She stood there for a minute before summoning up her strength and straightening her posture. "We'll have to summons the sheriff. I want him to see this so there is no doubt that we were defending ourselves," she said.

"We could bury the body and I could sneak his horse into town. They'd never find him and would be none the wiser on what happened," Boone said.

"As tempting as that may be, I can't do that to his wife and children. They deserve to have his body and know what happened."

"I can't imagine him having a wife and kids."

"Nor I, but maybe he was different with them. Let's get home."

They rode double on Boone's horse to the house without much of anything to say. When Jenny came out onto the porch and found out what had happened, she got herself so worked up that she collapsed into a chair and pulled a handkerchief from inside her dress to mop her brow.

"I guess I should have known that fool Hunter wouldn't let this go. My baby almost got herself killed today," Jenny lamented.

"Jenny, I'm fine. There's no need to visit what might have happened. It serves no purpose. Your hero over there came through for me again," Flannery said with a nod toward Boone.

The comment stopped Jenny's distress long enough to make her smile. "I bet he thought twice about it though," she teased.

All of them laughed, letting go of the built-up tension they were all feeling.

"Boone, will you go get the sheriff? You have the only saddle at the moment and there's no point in me adjusting the stirrups for one ride," Flannery said.

"I'll be happy to do that. I best be going so we don't run out of daylight," Boone replied. He mounted the horse and rode away.

"Aren't you glad I didn't let you run Boone out of here?" Jenny asked.

Flannery arched her eyebrows and tilted her head back. "Jenny Jackson, I've never known you to tell a lie in my life, but that certainly is a rewriting of history."

"I was the one that first came to appreciate him is all I meant. I kept you from acting on your more impulsive nature."

Shaking her head, Flannery said, "Yes, Jenny, you are certainly the calm and rational soul around here. I'd probably run around here like a crazed woman with unkempt hair if not for you. I'm going to wake Savannah from her nap and play with her for a while. Who knows how long all this business with the sheriff will take."

"Well then, you can deal with her if she gets fussy later on."

Flannery dashed past Jenny, ignoring the comment on her way to wake Savannah. She needed to feel the joy that her daughter's smiling face always brought to her. The mother and daughter were still playing in the yard when Boone returned with the sheriff. Flannery wasted no time on pleasantries before handing the child to Jenny and climbing up behind Boone in the saddle.

Boone first led the sheriff to the dead horse and pointed out the gun wound to the horse's hip before showing him where they had taken cover. They then rode to Hunter's body. The sheriff looked over the scene, glancing out toward the dead horse before commenting.

"Well, it doesn't take much of a detective to figure out that Hunter ambushed you two. He always was a damn fool – pardon my language. He was just like his old man, just not as smart. Boone, would you retrieve his horse and help me get Hunter across the saddle? I rue having to take the body to Joseph. That will not be pleasant," Sheriff Stout said.

Boone did as asked, and after they had the body tied in the saddle, the three of them stood silently. The sheriff seemed reluctant to leave.

"Sheriff, I want to thank you for your assistance and honesty. It would be easy to make this what it was not in order to appease Joseph Thurgood," Flannery said.

The sheriff made a sad smile. "Some may question my aptitude, but they can't question my integrity. I'm going to do my best to get it through Joseph's head that he best leave you alone, but I'd stay on my toes if I were you folks." With a nod of his head, the sheriff mounted up and rode away with Hunter's body in tow.

The Thurgood men and their ranch hands were putting their horses up for the day when Logan happened to glance up from the cinch he was unknotting. "Oh, God, no, not this," he blurted out.

The crew froze as they silently watched the sheriff ride up with the body.

"No, not Hunter," Joseph yelled as he barreled toward the body.

"I'm sorry to have to be the one to deliver him to you," the sheriff said, climbing down from his horse.

"What in the hell happened?" Joseph gently lifted his son's head and saw the bullet hole. The sight caused him to turn away and shudder.

"He tried to ambush Flannery Vogel and her ranch hand. He wasn't a good enough shot to get the job done."

Joseph eyed the sheriff, skepticism written on his face. "And how do you know that? Are you just taking their word?"

"I can take you there tomorrow and show you if you like. Hunter was on the Vogel property, hiding on a hillside. He shot a horse in the ass that Flannery was riding as they tried to escape. There is just no logical way to surmise that they instigated the shooting."

"So I suppose you're going to let them get by with killing my son."

"Joseph, it was self-defense. I'm telling you right now that you'd better leave them alone. I'll come after you if something bad happens to that family. God knows that woman has already been through enough. It'll be your ruin."

Emma Thurgood walked out of her house and spotted her son's body draped across the saddle. She began screaming uncontrollably, prompting Logan to run to his mother just as she collapsed onto the porch.

"Momma, let's get you in the house," Logan said. He helped his mother to her feet.

"No. No, I will not," Emma said. She willed herself to have the strength to march toward her husband.

"Momma, please don't," Logan hollered.

"You really did it this time. You finally managed to get one of your sons killed," Emma yelled.

"Emma, I didn't have anything to do with this. I told Hunter to leave the Vogel woman alone," Joseph protested.

"Maybe this time, but you're the one that taught him all your conniving ways, how to take what you want, and not worry about who gets hurt. Well, this time, it was one of your own. You'll have to live with this the rest of your miserable life. I can't imagine the pain Jill and the children will feel when you get to bring them this news. You might as well have been the one to put the bullet in Hunter."

Logan grabbed his mother's arm and started leading her away. "Let's go inside. You need to calm down before your heart acts up," he said.

Joseph stomped his foot. His face looked to be a cross between profound loss and rage with its red hue, and his eyes glaring but pooling with tears. "Woman, you have no call to talk to me that way. I've provided you with a wonderful life."

Emma looked over her shoulder at her husband. "Joseph Thurgood, I hope you rot in hell," she shouted.

Chapter 10

By the time the sun had risen enough to recognize the shape of objects in the yard, Boone was ready to go to town to purchase some weapons. As leery as he felt about leaving the ranch, he saw no other option. He left for Trinidad, and was waiting by the door of the gun shop when the owner arrived to open the business.

After the gunsmith recovered from his initial fear of getting robbed, he warmed up considerably when Boone dropped onto the display case a pouch of gold coins that Flannery had retrieved from a stash that she kept hidden in the house. Boone quickly picked out a new Winchester '73, a Colt Frontier, and a Sharps Model 1874 in a .45-70 caliber. He also bought enough ammunition to engage in a prolonged battle. With the goods paid for in full, the gunsmith gladly helped Boone carry the purchases to the wagon.

Boone fidgeted in the wagon seat all the way home and didn't relax until he saw that everyone was safe. He quickly set up targets with plans for some practice, but found that Jenny balked at the notion. She couldn't bring herself to shoot a gun no matter how much coaxing Boone and Flannery did. Boone finally contented himself with teaching her how to load the Winchester rifle. The old woman proved adept at the task, and in no time, she could fill the gun with cartridges as quickly as Boone could.

With Savannah in tow, Jenny retreated inside the house when the time came for the shooting.

"So, have you ever shot a gun before or was pointing it at me as close as you've ever came to using one?" Boone asked.

"Jimmy practiced with me a couple of times. I sure wouldn't have missed hitting you that day," Flannery shot back.

Boone grinned and nodded his head before proceeding to show her how to hold and aim the gun as if this was her first time using a weapon. When they were ready to shoot, they used the buckboard wagon to steady themselves to aim at the targets Boone had set up at thirty paces. Flannery tentatively took her first couple of shots, and then squeezed off five rounds as quickly as she aimed. Boone then took his turn at his target. He calmly and swiftly fired seven shots.

"Let's go see what damage we did," Boone said. He flashed a boyish grin.

They walked to the feed sacks that Boone had marked with a bullseye, and found that Flannery had hit the sack every time. Her shots were all vertically within eight inches of the mark and within a couple of inches horizontally. One shot had even hit the mark. Boone's volleys had either hit the bullseye or were no more than an inch away from center.

"That's pretty good shooting for someone that has only shot a gun a couple of times," Boone said. "You would certainly take down a man."

"Nothing compared to you."

"Well, I've probably shot enough cartridges to fill this wagon. That does make a difference."

"I suppose it does," Flannery said. She reached out and took Boone by the hand. She could see that her action caught him by surprise to the point that she thought he even flinched a little. "Do you think we can really defend ourselves?"

Boone looked around the yard of the home to survey the layout before answering. "Jimmy constructed a well-built home and he positioned it perfectly. Nobody could overrun us without paying a very heavy price. So, yes I think we can defend ourselves in your house, but we can't stay in there all the time. That's my main concern," he replied.

With her lips pursed, Flannery nodded her head. "I appreciate your honesty. I guess we can work on the corral for the next few days and see what happens."

"That's along the lines I was thinking. There's no need to worry yourself until there's something to worry about. Nothing good comes from it."

"I suspect you are right. I'm going to check on Savannah and then we can get busy," Flannery said. She released Boone's hand and marched toward the house.

Boone, looking dumbfounded, watched Flannery walk away. He just never knew what to expect from the woman. When she had grabbed his hand, he'd almost yanked it away because the act had startled him so badly. He wiped the perspiration lingering on his palm onto his trousers. He wasn't sure if the moisture was his sweat or Flannery's, but at least one of them had been perspiring for sure.

After Boone retrieved the posthole digger from the barn and headed toward the corral to begin digging another posthole, Flannery emerged from the house with Savannah.

"Boone, someone here wants to spend some time with you, and in light of the situation, I don't have the heart to say no. And besides that, I need to calm Jenny down before she pops a cork. She's as worried today as she was optimistic yesterday. Do you mind?" Flannery asked.

"I don't mind at all. I'd take spending time with Savannah over digging holes any old day of the week," Boone replied.

Savannah ran off the porch toward Boone as Flannery returned into the home. Boone grinned at the child before running and disappearing behind a large maple tree in the yard.

"Yoo-hoo," he called out.

With a giggle, Savannah pursued Boone. She ran after him and tried to catch him as he circled around the tree. She paused to rip a chunk of bark from the trunk before resuming her pursuit.

"Yoo-hoo."

Savannah caught sight of Boone, and with a laugh, she hurled the piece of bark at him before making a dash toward the house. Boone chased after her and lifted her high in the air, prompting a fit of giggles.

"Do it again. Do it again," Savannah pleaded.

When Flannery finally came out of the house, the two were still playing their game. Both were sweaty and out of breath from their exertions.

"I'm not paying you to wear yourself out playing with my child," Flannery teased.

Boone hoisted Savannah up into his arms and started walking toward Flannery.

"I think this child could run with a herd of mustangs and keep up," he said.

"You're not telling me anything that I don't already know."

"How's Jenny?"

"I think I have her calmed down some. Savannah can occupy her now that you have her all wound up."

"Savannah's probably ready for a nap."

"I seriously doubt that. Let's get to work. I know you have to be thinking that Savannah got her fun side from her daddy," Flannery said. She took Savannah from Boone and started walking toward the house, leaving him hesitant to even attempt a response.

∞

Joseph Thurgood had spent most of the morning piddling in the barn to avoid his wife, who wouldn't look or speak to him. She was too busy taking care of Hunter's wife, Jill, and their two children, Carson and Lisa, anyway. He'd sent all his ranch hands and his sons out to tell neighbors of Hunter's death and of the wake to be held the following day. As Joseph paced up and down the barn hallway, he occasionally looked out the doorway, expecting to see the undertaker at any moment returning Hunter's body. The mortician had promised the previous evening when he'd received the body that he would have Hunter home by noon, fully embalmed and his face repaired.

The ranch hands began drifting back in, and then Logan and Elliot returned. By then, Joseph had worked himself into a lather waiting for the body to be returned. The men all stood around looking at each other as they waited for orders.

"Pa, what do you want us to do?" Logan asked.

"You and your brother need to come into the house with me until they bring your brother back home. The rest of you are done for the day. I hope you all will pay your respects tomorrow at the wake. It would mean a lot to my wife. Then we're going to bury Hunter on Sunday, but come Monday, I'm telling you right now, I expect all of you to play your part in getting our pound of flesh. Nobody kills a Thurgood without retribution," Joseph said, his eyes flashing a maddened fire.

"Pa, getting revenge isn't going to bring Hunter back. We would have done the same thing they did to Hunter if they had attacked us. And there is a child involved. Do you really want that kind of thing on your conscience?" Logan asked.

"I don't know where I went wrong with raising you. You don't even deserve to wear the Thurgood name. We have to defend that name to keep our respect in the community. What would people think if we were to let Hunter's death pass without some revenge? They'll believe we're weak and who knows who will be coming after us if we don't," Joseph bellowed.

Logan shook his head in disbelief. At times like this, he wondered if he was the only sane man in his family or if maybe he was just too weak and passive to be a real man.

Elliot turned toward his brother, his face red and his forehead wrinkled in rage. "Hunter was always right about you. You have no guts."

"Oh, shut up, Elliot. You're as fragile as an egg. If Pa and Hunter hadn't always coddled you, you would have cracked a long time ago," Logan shot back.

"That's enough from both of you," Joseph warned.

Logan decided to make one last-ditch effort to reason with his father. "You heard what the sheriff said. If we kill Flannery, we're all going to go to jail. Sheriff Stout wasn't just talking," Logan warned.

"He has to have some evidence to get a conviction. I don't plan for there to be anything of the kind. And I can afford lawyers for all of us. Quit your worrying."

Logan grabbed his father by the arm and started marching him out of the barn. Joseph yanked his arm free of his son's grasp, but kept walking with him until they were out of earshot of the others.

"You always said that the only true secret is the one that one person is keeping. Do you really think that one of those five ranch hands won't spill his guts when the sheriff comes threatening him with a choice between freedom or a stretched neck?" Logan asked.

"I don't care at this point."

Before the conversation could go any further, the sight of the undertaker's wagon came into view.

"Go get your brother. You two can help carry the coffin into the house," Joseph said. He marched off to meet the mortician.

The Thurgood men, along with the undertaker and his assistant, carried the casket into the house and placed it on a low table. All of the family stood around in the room, looking uncomfortable and as if they didn't know what they should do.

"Would you like to view Hunter before I leave?" the undertaker whispered to Joseph.

Joseph looked around the room, unsure of what to say. His wife took the two small children by their hands and began walking them toward the kitchen.

"Someone come relieve me after they've had their time with Hunter," Emma said before exiting the room with her grandchildren.

Undertaker Mars opened the lid to the casket, prompting Hunter's wife, Jill, to begin sobbing hysterically. Logan, who had always gotten along with his sister-in-law far better than he had with his brother, rushed over to comfort her as the others stared at the corpse.

The undertaker had puttied in the bullet hole in Hunter's cheek and then used makeup in an attempt to cover the repair and bruises. The cosmetics made Hunter look like a ghost ready to jump up and haunt the house.

As Logan patted Jill's back, he glanced over at his father. For the first time ever, he thought of his pa as an old man. Joseph looked ashen and tired, as if a gust of wind would send him toppling onto the fine carpet. Logan had figured out as a young child that Hunter was his father's favorite. His brother was the one son that his old man would be lost without his presence. Logan wondered how far the great Joseph Thurgood would go in the name of revenge for his chosen.

When Jill had calmed herself some, Logan went to relieve his mother of watching the children.

"Momma, prepare yourself. In fact, you just might want to remember Hunter how he was," Logan said.

His mother nodded her head as she contemplated her son's advice. "No, I have to do it or the wondering will drive me insane."

Logan nodded his head that he understood before turning his attention to his six-year-old nephew and four-year-old niece.

Emma dawdled back to the front room and marshaled her courage to glance down at Hunter's body. A flood of memories came rushing back to her of when Hunter had been a young child. He'd been such a sweet little boy back then before his father's influence had swayed him to become the man he was. After Elliot had been born, she had almost divorced her husband.

By then, Joseph was a different man from the one she had married. As she gazed down at the lifeless body of her son, she wondered if the decision not to end the marriage would go down as the biggest mistake of her life. She turned and pointed her finger at her husband. "If there is one more drop of bloodshed around here, I will divorce you this time. You had better leave Mrs. Vogel and her poor child alone – and I mean what I say."

Chapter 11

Wendell Starr didn't know what to make of his invitation to Hunter's wake. Logan had assured him that he would be welcome and that his father wanted to let bygones be bygones, but the idea of a visit to the Thurgood ranch after their standoff still made him uncomfortable. That day had proven to be a mistake for which he truly regretted his actions. And while he had never particularly cared for Hunter, his death, nonetheless, troubled him. In Wendell's advancing age, he had become keenly aware of death lurking right outside his door.

As Wendell sat down at his desk and leaned back in his chair, he began to reminisce on his life. In his time, he'd done his fair share of evil things. Sometimes, he even wondered if Austin's condition could be the result of the son paying for the sins of the father. Truth be told, he very well might have killed Anderson Clark if he hadn't been able to bully the man into selling his ranch, just as he knew Joseph had killed Simon in a similar circumstance. Wendell pulled a cigar from his humidor and bit the cap off it. He studied the stogie, wondering if there still might be time left in his life to repent of his sins. With the strike of a match, he lit his cigar and made a vow to himself that he would become a better person. He puffed on the stick until he got it burning satisfactorily and then went to find Austin and Calvin.

Wendell found his son and son-in-law in the barn, feeding the horses. "I've decided to go to the wake. Calvin, I figure you could run home to change clothes and then we would head over to the Thurgood ranch. Austin, you don't have to go if you don't want to," he said.

Austin hadn't had a drink since the day Wendell had a talk with him in the barn. The only problem was, without the alcohol to take the edge off, Austin proved to be more high-strung and easy to agitate than ever. Wendell sometimes wished he could control his son's drinking so that he could find a happy medium between his current state and falling down drunk.

"I think I should make an appearance," Austin said. He then stared up into the rafters to watch a swallow flying about the barn.

Calvin became distracted for a moment as he watched his brother-in-law lose himself in the flight of a bird. He let out a sigh before turning his attention toward Wendell. "I would imagine that Kelly will want to go with us since she knows Jill," he said.

"That's fine. I don't see my daughter enough as it is."

"I'll get back here as quickly as I can," Calvin said. He hastily departed.

Wendell took Austin by the arm. "Let's go get cleaned up and changed," he said.

By the time Calvin returned with his wife, Wendell and Austin had hitched the four-seater carriage to a team of horses and were waiting. The family headed for the Thurgood ranch while Kelly, the loquacious member of the family, chatted away the time. For the first time in a long time, Austin didn't seem irritated by his sister's presence and managed to carry on a conversation with her.

As the carriage headed up the road leading to the house, Austin began to fidget in his seat. Beads of sweat popped up on his forehead and his skin paled. "I, I, I should have stayed home," he stammered.

Kelly patted her brother's leg. "You can do this. You'll be fine. Just concentrate on talking to people. You don't have to view the body."

Austin nodded his head, but didn't seem reassured.

The family arrived at the Thurgood ranch and were welcomed into the home. They entered the room where the wake was being held, and found it packed with area ranchers and a large number of townsfolk that had come to pay their respects. Wendell led the way toward the Thurgood family and began offering his condolences. Austin managed to pay his respects before spying a childhood friend and darting off to talk to him.

After Wendell viewed the body, he sidled up to Logan. "May I have a word with you?" he asked.

"Sure. Let's head toward the back," Logan replied.

After the two men had moved to the rear of the room and as far away from everyone as possible in the cramped quarters, Wendell said, "I've been thinking a lot about Hunter's death. I truly am saddened by the whole affair. It is my wish that there not be any bad blood between the families. I should have never accused your father of killing Simon the other day."

"Thank you. I wish for the same thing."

"Logan, I really hope your father doesn't retaliate against Flannery. If one more rancher is killed, there's likely going to be an all-out range war. Ranchers are going to start shooting first and asking questions later. They'll be as nervous as a cat in a rocking chair factory."

"Momma and I are doing our best to stop him, but you know how he is. I can't make any promises. Hunter was his favorite, and he's never listened to me anyway.

In fact, I'd go as far as to say he's ashamed to have me for a son."

Wendell nodded his head. "Sometimes the relationship between a father and son can be difficult. I know from whence I speak. You've tried to stop him. That's all I can ask for."

As Wendell finished speaking, he watched as Austin moved toward the coffin. His son stood there viewing the body for a moment and then began tottering. Wendell darted toward his son, only to see him fall into the casket and then slump to the floor. The commotion caused people to scurry out of the way and stare at the unconscious Austin.

Kelly was the first to reach her brother. She tapped on his cheek. "Austin, wake up. Austin, wake up. You've fainted."

Austin's eyes shot open, and he looked around the room in confusion before realizing where he was. "They shot him in the face. My God, this is just like the war. Do you know how many men I've seen with their faces blown off?" he hollered.

"Let's get you out of here and into some fresh air," Kelly said.

Wendell and Calvin helped Austin to his feet.

"Please take him outside. I'll join you in a moment," Wendell said.

Once Kelly and Calvin had guided Austin out of the room, Wendell walked over to Joseph and Emma.

"I'm truly sorry for this. This proved to be just too much for Austin. I should have known better than to let him come. My deepest condolences," Wendell said.

Joseph nodded his head. "We all have our crosses to bear. I hope Austin gets to feeling better."

Emma reached out and took Wendell's hand. "Thank you for coming. God bless," she said.

Wendell made a faint smile before quickly departing.

On the ride back to their ranch, Austin babbled the whole way about the carnage he had witnessed during the war, giving details he had never spoken of before that day. Any attempts to calm him down were thwarted by his undeterred talking over the top of any other voice.

When they reached home, Wendell poured his son a generous glass of whiskey with the hopes that the liquor would calm him enough to rest. Austin cradled the glass in his hands as if he was protecting an egg. He guzzled down the alcohol and fell asleep on the couch in short order.

"I'd give anything to have my old Austin back," Wendell mused.

"Daddy, that's never going to happen. This has been going on far too long and getting worse by the year. We just have to accept Austin for who he is," Kelly said.

"Oh, I know, but I worry where all this is leading. And for the record, I can still yearn for the old days if I want to," Wendell said and then dropped into a chair.

∞

The stream of visitors to the wake had finally run its course. Only a couple of ranchers were still there talking to Joseph. With the welcomed lull, Logan slipped into the kitchen to find his mother.

"Momma, I'm exhausted. I'm going to head on home," Logan said.

"Won't you stay for dinner? We'll never be able to eat all this food that people have brought us," Emma said.

"I would but I just want to go home. This has been a long day."

"All right, then. I'll see you in the morning." Emma leaned over and kissed Logan on the cheek.

As Logan headed for the front door, he gave a wave to his brother and father. He mounted his horse, and after riding out of sight of the house, he turned toward the Vogel ranch with his horse gaiting at a lope.

Boone and Flannery were about ready to call it a day. They had all the fence posts set into the ground and had begun nailing up the boards between the posts when Flannery glanced up the road and saw a rider approaching.

"Someone's coming," she said.

They both grabbed the rifles they kept handy nearby and watched the rider slowly coming toward the house.

"I believe that's Logan Thurgood," Flannery said.

Boone squinted his eyes and studied the rider. "I believe you are right."

"I can't imagine why he is paying us a visit. Why would a Thurgood show up here now?"

When Logan was within shouting distance, he called out, "I'm not wearing a sidearm." He lifted the reins high so that his hands were in view as he rode into the yard.

In a gesture of good faith, Boone and Flannery walked over to meet their visitor with their rifles slung over their shoulders.

"Logan, I have no idea why you are here, but Hunter never gave us a choice but to shoot him. He tried to kill us," Flannery said.

"That's what the sheriff told us. I don't doubt the accuracy of his findings. Pa told Hunter to leave you alone, but he tended to do whatever he pleased. He had it out for you," Logan replied.

"Then why are you here?"

"My momma and I are doing our best to keep Pa from seeking revenge, but honestly, I have my doubts we will succeed. If we fail, he plans on attacking you on Monday."

A little gasp escaped Flannery and she nervously rubbed her lips.

Boone took a step forward. "And why are you telling us this?" he asked.

"Because I've never had a taste for bloodshed, especially when it comes to retaliating for an act of self-defense."

"Even for your own brother?"

"You saw how Hunter was. He's just like my pa. They think they can take whatever they want. I personally think we have all the land we need. I guess I'm just cut from a different cloth."

Boone pushed his hat off his forehead and rubbed his brow. "You realize this information could get your family killed, don't you?"

"Sure, I do. Hell, it's liable to get me killed. I'll probably have to ride with them. I just know what my conscience can and cannot bear."

"Seems to me that you're old enough to decide things for yourself. Why would you ride with them if you don't believe in what you are doing?"

Logan let out a little snort. "Families are complicated things. I bet every man alive has done something for his family where he thought they were all crazier than a ghost under a full moon. I have at least put things on the level for you."

Flannery had managed to regain her composure. She stepped forward and patted the neck of Logan's horse. "We are so grateful for the warning. I'm sorry you have been put in such a quandary."

Logan snorted again. "I put myself in this quandary years ago when I let my pa bully me out of going to college. I wanted to study philosophy. Can you believe that? A rancher from Colorado wanting to study philosophy – now that's something. No wonder Pa threw a fit. I have to go." He swung his horse around and rode away.

Boone and Flannery stood there looking at each other.

"That was certainly unexpected," Boone said.

"Yes, it was. I actually feel sorry for Logan. He's trapped in a family that he doesn't fit in any better than a foot in a too small shoe," Flannery said.

"He seems like a decent enough fellow, but he needs to take charge of his life if he isn't happy. Nobody can do that for him."

"I guess you can relate. At least you had Jimmy."

Boone sighed and smiled. "That's all true. I did have Jimmy. Well, at least we know what to expect."

"I'm not sure the knowing makes it any easier. I'm going to worry myself sick between now and Monday."

"Worrying won't change one thing. It's just a complete waste of time. At least we'll be prepared and I'll have time to sight the Sharps in tomorrow."

"Boone, I'm sorry you had to get into this mess."

"Don't be. I'm just sorry I didn't know of Jimmy's death so that I could get here a lot sooner for you. I owed Jimmy that much."

"Do you think we'll be all right?"

Boone forced a smile. "I think we'll be just fine."

Chapter 12

On Monday morning, well before the first light of dawn, Boone, Flannery, and Jenny were already up and dressed. Jenny busied herself with frying eggs and bacon, and had biscuits baking in the oven. Boone and Flannery were checking the guns and going over their plans one more time. All were trying to be quiet in order not to wake Savannah. All of the anxiety in the household had made the child fussy on Sunday to the point that even an offer by Boone to give her a horseback ride had been met with rejection and tears. None of them wanted to deal with that at such an early hour.

"Breakfast is ready," Jenny whispered as she poured coffee into the cups.

Boone was the first to the table and scooped out a generous portion of scrambled eggs, grabbed three biscuits, and piled his plate with bacon. Flannery and Jenny took much smaller portions. As Boone attacked his food as if he were a starved man, Flannery stared at her plate, and Jenny picked at her food.

"I don't see how you can have such an appetite at a time like this," Flannery finally said with a slight exasperation to her voice.

"Flannery, I've already told you that worrying doesn't accomplish a thing. It just doesn't. Whatever is about to happen is going to happen one way or the other, no matter how you feel about it," Boone replied.

"I still don't see how you can be so cavalier. Maybe you just got used to this kind of thing while being a Texas Ranger."

"I wouldn't say you ever get used to it, but you do learn how to accept things. A man would go crazy worrying all the time while we were out there fighting the Indians. I'd wither away to nothing if I didn't eat any more than you have the last couple of days. Speaking of which, you can't get any skinner than you are or you're liable to blow away."

"I beg your pardon. I'll remind you to keep your opinions to yourself," Flannery said, her voice rising in indignation.

The exchange caused Jenny to break into a big smile for the first time that morning. "That's exactly what I tell her all the time. A man would lose her in the sheets," she said.

Flannery's face turned beet red as she glowered at the black woman. "Jenny Jackson, I won't have such talk at my table. You need to mind your manners," she fumed.

Much to Flannery's chagrin, Jenny responded with a belly laugh that proved contagious for Boone. As he cackled, he had to set his coffee cup down to keep from spilling it. His eyes began to water and he had to wipe them.

"If you two wake up Savannah, Joseph Thurgood will be the least of your worries," Flannery threatened as she stood to carry her uneaten plate of food and cup to the sink.

After Boone regained his composure, he said, "We best take our places. Jenny and Savannah will be safe in Savannah's room. I'm not worried about a bullet traveling that far. Flannery, go to your room and watch the barn. I still think they'll come from the front at first light, but I could be wrong. They might come from two directions. If I start shooting, don't come unless I call you."

Flannery was still miffed from the laughter at her expense. She grabbed the Winchester and stalked off toward her bedroom. "I'm not a simpleton. You don't have to tell me the same thing ten times," she muttered as she went.

Boone and Jenny smiled knowingly at each other.

"She never could tolerate laughter at her expense. Nothing has changed there," Jenny said.

"She's kind of cute when she's mad. At least then, she doesn't look as if she's just waiting around to die like on most days."

"You've been good for her. You keep her busy and on her toes. She needed that."

"I just hope I can get us through this mess. Better get ready, I guess. First light is just beyond the horizon."

Jenny walked over to Boone and patted his back. "I have full faith in you and the Lord to get us through this. God bless you," she said before heading toward Savannah's bedroom.

∞

After Hunter's funeral, Joseph Thurgood had made it known to his sons and ranch hands that he intended to meet them on Monday in the bunkhouse an hour earlier than usual. To his surprise, when he walked into the building, he found that not only was everybody up, but they were ready to ride.

"I appreciate all of you and your willingness to help settle this score. It means a lot to me and I know it would to Hunter, too. If we succeed, you'll all receive a bonus. We just have to remember to keep our mouths shut afterward," Joseph said.

Logan looked around the room trying to gauge the mood of the men. He quickly came to the conclusion that everyone was too scared of his old man to show anything but blind loyalty. While he inhaled loudly, he steeled himself before speaking. "Pa, I'm begging you to reconsider doing this. It's just plain wrong. Hunter was a damn fool, and you know it. We would have defended ourselves in the same situation, and you know that, too. And if that isn't enough to make you change your mind, you better be thinking about the sheriff. He's not playing around."

Joseph had stood silently as his son spoke, his face turning red and scrunching up into pure anger. "How dare you disparage your brother. At least he had the guts to fight for what he wanted. You've always been a coward and you'll die one. Right or wrong has nothing to do with this. We avenge the death of a Thurgood – plain and simple," he roared.

"So you're going to murder a woman and a child?" Logan yelled back.

"I have no intentions of killing the child."

"No, you'll just leave her a damn orphan. What a life that'll be."

"Maybe you can adopt her. Nursing children is more to your true calling anyway."

Logan couldn't help but wince at his father's slight. The words stung. He'd always been a loyal son to the point of giving up on his own dreams to please his pa, and now to be treated so contemptuously proved to be the last straw. From now on, he'd prove his courage by being the one brave enough to think for himself. "I won't be part of this. You can call me a coward, but actually I just have the moral courage to do what's right instead of kowtowing to you."

Joseph stood there for a moment, his body trembling in rage, before speaking. At that moment, he loathed his son more than he thought humanly possible. The notion crossed his mind to kill Logan right there on the spot. "You make me ashamed to call you my son, and I wish you'd never been born. You're dead to me. I'm leaving now. Any man worth his salt can come with me."

As the men filed out of the room, Logan stood there not knowing what to feel. His anger was fading away, but the hurt and need to cry still lingered. A deep sadness began to sink into his bones like a cold winter chill. The accumulated resentment for a lifetime of blind loyalty had led to this moment and now there was no return. He stood there for a few minutes before walking to the door and listening to the hoofbeats fading into the dark.

By the time Joseph and his crew neared the Vogel ranch, the morning had lightened from a cloudy black night to a gray where objects were becoming visible. Joseph called out to his men to stop as they reached a tree line a couple of hundred yards from the Vogel home. "We're going to walk in from here. There are plenty of mature trees to hide behind in the front yard. Now I need you all to listen up good. I want Flannery Vogel and her hired man both dead. I expect the widow will be coming out of the house and the ranch hand from the bunkhouse. We'll have to wait until both are out in the open before we fire. So just be patient. They won't be expecting us at this early hour. Pull your bandanna up over your nose. Come on now. Just follow me," he lectured as he began his march toward the Vogel home.

The first signs of movement off in the distance had Boone squinting to focus his sight. He'd been staring into the gray morning for so long that his eyes burned. With a couple of blinks, the sight of men scrambling toward the yard came clearly into view. In the poor light, Boone wasn't exactly sure of how many there were but he counted four for sure. He raised the Winchester to the window's edge and looked down the barrel. The early morning provided just enough light to see his bead. As he waited for the men to get close enough for a shot, the thought crossed his mind that Logan might be out there. He really did not want to kill him. After taking aim, Boone squeezed the trigger and the roar of the gun ruptured the serenity of the morning. The men all froze in unison, and then the targeted man slumped to the ground.

"Run for cover," a voice bellowed.

Pandemonium ensued as the men dashed for the safety of the trees in the yard. Boone took aim at another man, but knew he missed as soon as he fired the round. The men made it to cover and began returning fire. With the sound of breaking glass, the window where Boone was stationed became the first causality in the home. He exchanged gunfire in hopes of preventing the men from advancing any closer to the house.

"Flannery, I believe they're all in front of us. I think I could use your help," Boone hollered.

"I wondered if you were ever going to call," Flannery said. She ran across the room and took a position at a window.

"Just be careful."

The gunfight continued with Thurgood's men peppering the house with bullets. Savannah could be heard squalling from her room as Jenny belted out black spiritual songs, one after the other. Boone and Flannery found it impossible to take anything more than potshots for fear of getting hit by the barrage of return fire.

"We're never going to be able to get a decent shot," Flannery exclaimed.

"We're fine. As long as we keep them honest, they can't rush us. They won't stay here all day. They weren't prepared for this and will run out of cartridges," Boone assured her.

Flannery popped up to take a shot just as a bullet tore into the windowsill. She let out a yelp and fell backward onto her back. The sight of her sprawled out on the floor caused Boone to freeze in a panic for a moment before he sprang into action. He ran across the room to her, slid into a sitting position, and scooped her up into his arms.

"Where are you hit?" he hollered.

"My hand. I can't bear to look. Is it mangled?"

Boone grabbed her by the wrist and saw a two-inch splinter imbedded into the back of her hand. He yanked the wood free, prompting another yelp. "It's a big splinter. You should be fine. Here, wrap it with this. I have to get back to the window or they'll overrun us," he said. He untied the kerchief around his neck and handed it to her.

"I'm sorry. I'm being a big ole baby."

"You are nothing of the kind. That probably hurt more than a bullet. Just a lot less damage," Boone said. He took Flannery's place at the window and fired a round.

The gunfire continued until the shooters began retreating. The men's bandanna-covered faces and the nature of the shooting exchanges hadn't allowed Boone an opportunity to get a clear look at any of them. He remained sitting at the window, watching as they hightailed it away. When the intruders came upon the downed man, they stopped and retrieved him before resuming their escape.

With time to catch his breath, Boone started fuming over what had happened. He marched over to the Sharps rifle and shoved a cartridge into the chamber. After returning to the window, he took aim on a man that looked to be too short and thick to be Logan. He gently squeezed the trigger. Inside the house, the gun sounded unbearably loud as the roar bounced off the walls. A moment later, one of the assailants flopped to the ground.

"We won that round," Boone said. With the culprits retreating, he turned his attention back to Flannery.

Flannery sat with her back to the wall, holding her wounded hand against her breasts. She looked pale and as if the fight had all been knocked out of her. "Thank you," she quietly said.

"You did your part. I'm telling you right now that I think you have a lot of grit. You'd make a Texas Ranger proud to serve with you."

"Please go check on Savannah and Jenny."

Boone walked to the bedroom and found Jenny rocking Savannah. Both of them looked scared out of their wits and as if they'd cried themselves out.

"Everything is fine. Flannery took a splinter to the hand. You might need to doctor her."

Jenny shot out of the rocking chair and passed Savannah to Boone before rushing out of the room. For the next couple of minutes, Boone soothed the child before carrying her to the front of the house. He found Flannery sitting at the kitchen table while Jenny applied iodine to the wound.

"I'll tell you what, that hand is going to be mighty sore for the next couple of days," Jenny said. "It missed the bone, but went deep into the muscle. Praise Jesus we're all still living."

"Are you in much pain?" Boone asked.

Flannery didn't seem to hear him. She smiled at Savannah. "Come sit on my lap while Jenny wraps my hand. Your momma has an ouchy, but I'm a big girl."

Boone placed Savannah in Flannery's lap. He felt compelled to do something, and clumsily reached down and patted Flannery's back.

"You scared me," he said. "I was worried that Jenny and I wouldn't know what to do with ourselves if we didn't have you ordering us around."

Flannery glanced up and smiled before squeezing her mouth tightly shut. She looked as if she was on the verge of tears. "You are a brave man, Boone. We are blessed to have you here," she said.

"Yes, we are," Jenny chimed in.

Boone smiled sheepishly. "I hope you're right. I still fear I set all this in motion. Maybe if I hadn't been here, Hunter would have let things go. Anyway, I'm going to ride to town to tell the sheriff what happened. I wish I could have got a look at them so I could say positively that it was the Thurgoods even if I know it had to be. Were you able to recognize any of them?"

Flannery shook her head.

Jenny came barreling across the room. "You aren't going anywhere. You are going to stay right here and protect my babies. I'll go to town," she said.

Flannery looked toward the black woman. "Jenny, I don't know if that's a good idea. I'm not sure how the sheriff will react to hearing the news from you."

"I know what you're thinking, but the sheriff always speaks to me in a friendly way. I don't believe he has it in for us Negroes. It don't matter anyway because he will hear what I have to say no matter what color my skin is. I won't take no for an answer from him or you. Boone just needs to help me hitch the horses to the wagon," Jenny said.

With the realization that the battle was already lost, Boone saluted Jenny. "Yes, ma'am. Let's get those horses hitched."

Chapter 13

After the Thurgood crew lugged the bodies of the two dead ranch hands back to the horses, they stood with their hands braced against their knees and sucked in loud gulps of air as they struggled to catch their breaths. Joseph wobbled from his exertions and looked as if he could faint at any moment. When they finally recovered a bit, they tied the two men onto their saddles and wasted no more time in racing back toward the ranch. Joseph held his horse to a lope the whole way even as the animal tired and lathered up. Once home, he led the men straight through the open doors of the barn and into the hallway in hopes of avoiding detection by his wife.

Joseph did a quick sizing up of the men as they gathered around him. His son and ranch hands all looked bewildered. Their brows were furrowed in worry and the armpits of their shirts were soaked in nervous sweat. They kept wincing at the sight of the two bodies slung over the horses' backs. He realized he had no time to waste in taking charge of the situation before it spiraled out of control.

"You men need to listen up good. We don't have much time. You need to go to the shed and get the shovels and then take the bodies to Lonesome Valley and bury them deep. Dig the sod off first and put it to the side and then put it back last. After a couple of rains, nobody will ever know anyone is buried there. Take their horses into some heavy pines and shoo . . ."

"You mean to tell me that you want us to bury Hank and Jose in unmarked graves after they both worked for you for the last ten years? That's a hell of a way to pay respect for their loyalty to you," Barney interrupted.

"Unless you want to spend the next ten years in prison for attempted murder, I suggest that's what you do," Joseph yelled as he tried to stare Barney into submission with no success. "I'm not too sure we didn't hit the widow. She could be dead for all we know, and then it would be murder. Now shut up and do what you are told. Take the horses into some pines and shoot them. Nobody will be able to recognize them in a couple of days. Bring the tack back. The sheriff is going to be coming here, and we all need the same story. We'll say that Hank and Josie got gold fever and left for Comstock, Nevada. We spent the morning moving some herd from the west pasture up into the foothills. Any questions?"

"I don't like this at all," Barney said.

"Barney, I don't give a damn what you like. If we don't stick together, we'll all go down. There'll be a nice bonus for all of you for your loyalty. I'm sorry this didn't go as planned. For the life of me, I can't believe they were waiting for us. It was as if they knew we had this planned. I guess they figured I'd avenge Hunter's death and would be coming soon."

"What about Logan?" Elliot asked.

"Go see if he's still around here somewhere."

Elliot scurried out of the barn. He returned a few minutes later, out of breath from his jogging. "He's nowhere to be found," he said.

"I'll worry about him later. We'll just say he never showed up this morning and must be sick. I'm going to clean out Hank and Jose's belongings from the bunkhouse. Now get to work. You need to be back here by the time the sheriff gets here."

∞

Sheriff Stout, along with deputies Kenneth Lyons and Toby Hill, arrived at the Vogel ranch a couple of hours after Jenny had gone to retrieve the lawman. As the sheriff climbed off his horse, he let out a whistle and shook his head in dismay while surveying the gunfire damage to the home.

"Looks like a war," the sheriff said to himself as much as he did to his deputies.

Boone, with Savannah in his arms and Flannery by his side, walked out of the house to meet the lawmen.

"Thank you for coming," Flannery said.

The sheriff smiled. "I was too afraid of Miss Jenny not to come. That woman is downright persuasive and a force of nature. She said to tell you she was going to pick up some supplies before she headed back home. Seriously though, I'm sorry you had to endure this. Looks like you're lucky to only have a hand wound."

"Yes, we are. Boone had us ready. I don't know what we would have done without him."

Sheriff Stout noticed that Flannery seemed to be almost awestruck by her hired hand. He hadn't seen such personable behavior in her since Jimmy had died. Boone, on the other hand, looked embarrassed by the compliment.

"How were you so ready for them?" the sheriff asked Boone.

Until that moment, Boone hadn't thought about the possibility of having to implicate Logan for his warning. He had no intentions of doing such a thing if at all possible. "I had an inkling they'd attack at dawn. We were ready for them. I shot two of them, and I believe they're dead," he said.

The sheriff nodded his head as he glanced at the damage again. "I guess all that Texas Ranger training came in handy. Can you identify the men?"

Curling his lip in disgust, Boone shook his head. "No, they were wearing masks to hide their faces, and we weren't exactly keeping our heads popped up in the windows to get them blown off while we tried to get a gander either," he answered.

As Sheriff Stout stewed on the answer, he pulled a small bag from his vest pocket and extracted a piece of rock candy. Without seeking permission, he held the treat up to Savannah's lips and grinned as she eagerly mouthed it. "Are you sure you couldn't identify them?" he asked.

"No, I couldn't."

"Are you sure?"

"Sheriff, I know what you're wanting, and even though we know it was the Thurgoods, I won't lie about what I saw."

"Flannery, did you see them?" the sheriff asked in hopes she would give the answer he wanted.

"No, I wish I could have," she replied.

"There were seven of them," Boone added.

"That's interesting. I would have expected either three or eight. Somebody stayed behind. Anyway, if I see tracks that go from here to the Thurgood ranch, I'm arresting them for attempted murder. You folks should be safe."

Flannery reached out and touched the sheriff's arm. "Thank you so much for your help. You're an honor to your profession," she said.

"Just trying to do my job. You folks take care of yourselves."

The sheriff turned to walk away and then spun back around as he again reached for his bag of candy. He wanted to see the little girl smile one more time before he took his leave.

"Thank you," Savannah managed to say with her mouth full of candy.

"Aren't you a polite little thing," Sheriff Stout replied. He tipped his hat before he and the deputies rode away.

The tracks leading back to the Thurgood ranch were as easy to find as a beer in a saloon. In the escape, the horses had dug their hoofs into the ground and kicked up chunks of grass as they ran. As the lawmen neared the Thurgood home, Sheriff Stout pulled his rifle from its scabbard and ordered his deputies to do the same. They rode up to the house and found the men milling about the barn getting ready to break for lunch.

"Sheriff, what brings you out here?" Joseph greeted the lawman.

"I think you know darn well why I'm here," the sheriff replied.

"Can't say that I do."

"I want to talk to you in private," Sheriff Stout said. He turned to face his deputies. "Keep your eyes on all of them. If need be, shoot first and ask questions later."

"Whatever you want," Joseph replied and started walking away from his men.

The sheriff followed the rancher until they were out of earshot of the ranch hands.

"You tried to kill Flannery Vogel and Boone Youngblood this morning," Sheriff Stout accused.

"I have no idea what you are talking about. My men and I spent this morning moving cattle from our west pasture up into the foothills."

"Where are Hank and Jose?"

"Funny you should ask, but they got gold fever real bad and headed out for Comstock, Nevada to make their fortunes."

"I can't say I find anything amusing about any of this, but I do find it mighty coincidental that Boone shot two of the attackers and now you're down two men."

"What are the odds?" Joseph said as he stared the sheriff in the eye. "You can question my men if you don't believe me."

"Joseph, your tracks lead right from the Vogel ranch straight to here. You tried to kill them. You can't deny it."

"Probably wild mustangs running about. You know how they are."

"Yeah, I see shod mustangs every day. Give me a damn break. Where is Logan?"

"He must have been sick. He never showed up for work today. Certainly not like him."

"I would think you would've checked on him, especially since you've just lost a son."

"I planned on doing that right after lunch if he didn't show up by then."

The sheriff couldn't help but to show his agitation that the rancher had an answer for everything. His face began to get red and he rubbed the toe of his boot into the ground. Joseph had obviously taken the time to plan an answer for every scenario. "In other words,

Logan was the only Thurgood with enough of a conscience not to attack the widow," he growled.

"Did the widow or her ranch hand identify us?" Joseph asked in a smug tone.

The question gave the sheriff pause. "No," he finally replied.

"Then I suggest you quit wasting my time and get out of here."

Enraged by the rancher's behavior, the sheriff grabbed Joseph by the shirt and yanked him so that they were nose to nose. "Don't you ever tell me what to do again. You are not above the law, no matter how important you think you are. I'm going to talk to each one of your men individually. I'll shoot you if you give me a lick of trouble. Do you understand?"

The outburst caught Joseph so off guard that he was taken aback and didn't offer resistance. "Do what you have to do," he said.

By the time Sheriff Stout had finished interviewing all of the men, he had come to the conclusion that Joseph had already rehearsed the answers with his men. Their replies were so similar that they might as well have been reading from a script. The sheriff's agitation had grown with each interview until he was ready to give someone a good beating. He walked out of the barn and made a single nod of his head to his deputies. The well-trained lawmen raised their rifles and pointed them at the men.

"You are all under arrest for the attempted murders of Flannery Vogel and Boone Youngblood. Unfasten your gun belts and let them fall to the ground. Try anything and you'll die," the sheriff commanded.

Joseph stalked toward the sheriff. "You can't be serious. You don't have a thing to prove such accusations," he screamed.

"I have tracks to and from here to the Vogel ranch and I have two missing ranch hands that were killed today. I say I have all the evidence I need."

"You're nothing but a two-bit sheriff that holds his office by the grace of all of us ranchers. I'll have your job for this."

The sheriff forced a smile. "That may well be, but all the same, you're under arrest for attempted murder."

Chapter 14

Wendell had come to regret giving Austin the glass of whiskey after returning home from Hunter's wake. His son had stayed drunk ever since then. Even attempts to hide the liquor had proved fruitless as Austin apparently had alcohol stashed all over the ranch. Wendell and Calvin had tried talking to him to no avail, and had gone as far as recruiting Kelly to try to help with the situation, but her brother had bristled when she showed up to talk to him and he threw a screaming fit in order to end the conversation.

As Wendell sat at his desk and reminisced about happier times when his son and daughter were young and his wife was still alive, he glanced out the window and saw Austin stumbling out of the barn with his horse in tow. Wendell jumped up from his seat and scurried outside as fast as his sixty-one-year-old legs would allow. By the time he made it to his son, Austin had somehow managed to climb up onto the saddle of his horse and was about to ride away. With a quick swipe, Wendell snatched the reins out of his son's hands.

"Where do you think you're going?" Wendell asked.

"I'm headed to town," Austin replied in a voice that sounded amazingly clearheaded considering the way he had staggered out of the barn.

"Don't you think you're a little too drunk to be on top of horse? You're liable to fall off and break your neck."

"I can ride when I'm passed out. Staying in the saddle when you're in hand-to-hand combat, now that takes some doing."

Wendell shielded his eyes from the sun and slowly nodded his head as he looked up at Austin. "Your mind is always back at the war, isn't it?"

Austin shut his eyes as if he might take a nap on the spot. "Pretty much," he replied.

"Why don't you stay here with me? We could go fishing at the pond. The fish might be biting with sunset coming."

"Pa, I'm going to be forty years old this year. If I want to go to town, just let me. Please just hand me my reins."

Wendell stood there staring up at his son and wishing he had some magical words that would fix what ailed Austin. After handing over the reins, he turned to shuffle back toward the house. The sound of Austin's horse loping away filled him with as much loneliness as the first night after his wife died when he'd slept alone in the bed they'd shared for their whole marriage. His mind jumped to thoughts of his granddaughters, and as he climbed the stairs to the porch, he made a vow to spend some time with them. He needed to be with ones that were young enough that life hadn't yet soiled their minds.

Austin felt no hurry to get to town. He rode at an easy trot and even sang a couple of tunes just to occupy his mind for a few moments. If he thought too much, he'd have to figure out why he wanted to go to Trinidad in the first place. Normally, he hated being in crowds. Sometimes they even made him sick to his stomach, but for some reason for which he didn't want to understand, he needed to be in a saloon full of men that evening.

After arriving in town, Austin rode up and down the main street a couple of times as he vacillated on which saloon to visit. He finally tied his horse in front of the Cattleman's Saloon and marched through the door. The place was crowded with ranch hands from the various area ranches, and he had to maneuver through the men to get to the bar. He bought a bottle of whiskey and stood there sipping from his glass as he eavesdropped on others' conversations.

The only subject any of them seemed to be talking about was the news that Joseph Thurgood and his crew were all in jail for trying to kill Flannery Vogel. Most of the men seemed thrilled with the turn of events. The news troubled Austin as he assumed that Logan was also behind bars. Logan had always done right by him when others had treated him as if he were a leper.

"What do you think about old Thurgood getting locked up?" a man that Austin didn't know asked him.

Austin shrugged. "I can't say he's one of my favorite people, but I don't know any of the details about what happened."

"They say Thurgood, his sons, and his ranch hands ambushed Flannery Vogel. Her ranch hand shot two of them and now Thurgood has two of his men missing. He claims they left for Nevada. That's what I hear anyway. That ranch hand of hers must be something. That's three dead for Thurgood and zero for Vogel."

"I feel sorry for Logan. He's not like the rest of his family. I fear he got roped into something he didn't want any part in doing."

"Why do you care? Those Thurgoods are all alike. I wouldn't lose no sleep over any of them."

The condescending nature of the stranger hit Austin wrong. He didn't see why the world had to be so full of hate and loathing for one's fellow man. A moment of guilt gripped Austin for the way he'd treated Kelly on the last time they'd spoken to each other. With a scowl on his face, he shook his head in disgust. "Do you even know Logan?" he asked in an exasperated tone.

"I just know some of the ranch hands. They have plenty to say about the Thurgood bunch. Don't be acting so high and mighty with me. I'm entitled to my opinion."

"I'm just trying to tell you that Logan is different from the others."

"All right, you told me. Now I'll tell you something. I have no pity for that widow, either. No woman should be trying to run a ranch. It's pure folly is what it is. There'd be some more jobs around here for us ranch hands if she was gone. Nobody will work for her 'cause they know they're liable to get shot."

"I feel sorry for Mrs. Vogel. It took a real coward to kill her husband, and she's entitled to run the ranch that she owns as much as any man is."

"You're something else. Maybe you should be passing out meals at the orphanage. A man has to be tough to survive. I don't see how you're still standing."

"I've killed many a man in the war. Have you ever killed a man?" Austin shot back.

The stranger looked away and ignored the question.

Austin began scratching his face the way he always did when agitated. His actions left bright red marks on his cheek. In hopes of calming himself, he took a big gulp of the whiskey. As he savored the taste, somebody dropped a beer mug and the glass shattered with a loud crack. Austin ducked and then drew his revolver. He started shooting into the ceiling, sending patrons diving for cover.

"Don't anybody move or I'll kill you. You are all now prisoners of war of the United States of America. We have you surrounded. Everyone set their weapons on the ground. We don't wish for any more bloodshed. You'll be well taken care of," Austin yelled as he spun one direction and then another.

Sheriff Stout heard the shooting from the street and rushed into the saloon with his revolver in hand, finding everyone crouching on the floor except for Austin. Austin whirled toward him and took aim. Against the sheriff's better judgement, he held his fire.

The sheriff needed to catch his breath before speaking. He and Austin stood facing each other with guns drawn as he gasped for air. "Austin, what are you doing?" the sheriff asked in a conciliatory tone.

"We've taken all these Rebels captive, sir," Austin responded.

"Austin, the war has been over for a long time. You're back in Trinidad. I'm Sheriff Stout, remember?"

"Who are all these men then?" Austin surveyed the crouching cowboys.

"You are in the Cattleman's Saloon. They were just in here drinking beer, same as you."

Austin slowly looked around the room again. He colored in embarrassment before letting his gun sink to his side. The sheriff figured that the war veteran was regaining his senses and took a step toward him with his hand held out to collect the gun. Austin, with a crazed look that reminded the sheriff of a rabid dog, jerked his arm up and pointed the revolver back at Sheriff Stout.

"Sheriff, you'll have to kill me to get my gun," Austin threatened.

The first things that crossed the sheriff's mind were that Austin had addressed him by his title and that he was no longer delusional. He felt certain that Austin just wanted to die and hoped to get the sheriff to oblige his wish.

"Austin, I'm not going to kill you, and the last thing in the world that you want is to kill another person. You had a lifetime's worth of that in the war. Neither of us want any more death. Give me your gun and let's walk to the jail," Sheriff Stout pleaded.

Austin's body started trembling all over and a cry escaped him. His appearance brought to mind a young boy grieving over his dead dog. He gazed longingly at his gun, and then with dexterity that belied his drunken state, he twirled his revolver and reversed it so that it pointed away from the sheriff. Sheriff Stout reached out and disarmed him. He put his arm around Austin's shoulders and began to walk him out of the saloon.

"You should have killed the crazy bastard," the man that had been talking to Austin said.

Sheriff Stout spun around and crashed Austin's revolver into the man's head. The blow took the ranch hand to his knees and left him woozy. "Mind your own damn business," the sheriff said before resuming his walk with Austin.

As they were strolling down the street, Austin said, "You shouldn't have arrested Logan. I know he didn't want to be part of trying to kill Flannery and I'm sure he didn't shoot at them."

"I didn't arrest Logan. As far as I can tell, he wasn't with them. I went to his house and talked to him. He claims no knowledge of the plan. I think he's lying on that, but at least he stood up to Joseph and didn't take part in it. And don't you tell anyone that I said this, but I have a hunch he warned the widow, too. They were mighty prepared for an attack."

The news greatly lifted Austin's spirit and he even smiled. "That's a relief. I think Logan might be an angel sent down here to save us all."

Sheriff Stout raised his eyebrows and nodded his head to appease his companion. "Well, we need us some angels around here. Let's go have some coffee. You can't go around shooting up saloons anymore. You're liable to accidentally kill a whore or her customer, but we can have us a good talk about that later. You can sleep in a cell tonight."

Chapter 15

As Logan rode from his home to the ranch to check on his mother and do chores, he contemplated the state of his life. He didn't see any way he could continue working on the ranch if his pa somehow beat the charges against him. The notion that he'd have to find a new job filled him with dread even if he was miserable working with his father. He'd never had another job in his life. If his pa went to prison, he saw no choice but to run the ranch for his mother. He had no regrets over warning Flannery either, even if his actions could have gotten his father and brother killed. For reasons he didn't fully understand, he could no longer look away from his pa's misdeeds. One way or the other, he'd reached a crossroads in his life. The time had come to settle down and live a good clean life.

Logan was surprised to see his mother sitting in the swing on the veranda. She smiled and tapped on the seat to signal him to come sit beside her.

"How are you doing, Momma?" Logan asked as he climbed the stairs.

Emma let out a sigh and waited for Logan to sit down before she spoke. "I honestly can't say. I don't know what to think anymore. One son is dead, one is in jail with his pa, and you look like you have the weight of the world on your shoulders."

"Don't you worry about me. I'll be fine."

"Of course I'm going to worry about you. You're the only one around here I can talk to. I love all my sons, but you and I are cut from the same cloth. Hunter and Elliot take after their daddy."

"You know, as much as Hunter and I butted heads, I do miss him already."

"Of course you do – you are bound as brothers whether you like it or not. My heart is broken. I know you don't remember it, but Hunter was such a sweet boy when he was little. He was so protective of you back then. Joseph ruined him, and I couldn't or didn't stop it – I don't know which."

"Momma, you did your best for all of us. Hunter made his choice."

"I suppose, but it still hurts. I need to go over and check on Jill and the children. They're grieving bad. I worry about them."

"Jill is close to her family. That'll help some. And I'll be there for them. Are you really going to divorce Pa?"

Emma lowered her chin and rubbed her forehead. "No, I'm not. I'm forty-seven years old. What am I going to do with myself at that age? I made my bed a long time ago and there I'll stay, for better or worse."

Logan nodded his head as he studied on her words. "Pa's never going to forgive me for standing up to him and not riding with all of them to kill the widow. I'll stay around until he's back home, whether that's this week or in ten years, but after that, I'm done."

His mother made a sad smile, and placed her hand on top of his. "I think that's a wise decision as long as you remember to come visit your momma. You'll always be welcome here. I'll see to that much. Joseph will get out of this mess – you just wait and see. He always does. That's why I went to the bank yesterday. I transferred five thousand dollars into your account. I put money in

Jill's account, too. God knows that Joseph doesn't pay you enough to leave here."

"Momma, you can't do that. That's not mine to take, and Pa will be fit to be tied. That's a lot of money. You need it for the ranch. There's no telling what he'll do when he finds out."

"You let me worry about him. I'll be the one in control. I'll make him think I will leave if he fights me on the money. He already knows he's on thin ice with me. You've sacrificed enough in your life for the whims of Joseph Thurgood. I should have fought harder for you to go to college like you wanted. That's one of the biggest regrets of my life."

"That's all water under the bridge now. I should have stood up to him a long time ago. You know, you could come live with me. We'd both be free then."

Emma let out a small chuckle. "I'm not the woman you need to be sharing your home with. You need to go find you a nice girl and get yourself married. There's more to life than watching the south end of a cow."

"Thank you, Momma. I don't know how I would have ever made it without you. Why does life has to be so hard?"

"Because people make it hard. Most of them would rather be right, or rich, or who knows what, rather than happy."

∞

After saddling his horse, Wendell was ready to ride to Trinidad to try to find Austin. He felt worried sick about his son. The only thing keeping the rancher from total panic was that the sheriff hadn't showed up at the ranch to deliver bad news. Just as he mounted his horse, he spied Austin riding toward home. The old man tied his mount in front of the house and climbed the porch to wait for his son.

"Where in the hell have you been? I was just getting ready to go look for you. You had me worried sick," Wendell greeted.

"Sheriff Stout let me sleep off my drunkenness in his jail. I'm sorry I worried you, but it took me awhile to get up and going this morning. I shot up the Cattleman's Saloon last night. The sheriff was more than kind in his handling the situation. He could have justifiably killed me," Austin answered matter-of-factly.

Wendell rubbed his nose with his forefinger and furrowed his brow as he tried to decide what to make of Austin's pronouncement. His son seemed as lucid as he'd seen him in months, which made his news all the more puzzling. "I'm just glad you're safe," he finally said.

As the men talked, Calvin and some of the ranch hands came out of the barn and corral, and were standing around watching the father and son.

"We need to talk in private," Austin said.

"Tie your horse up and come on inside then." Wendell didn't bother to wait for his son, but turned and walked into the house.

Austin lumbered into the study and dropped into a chair.

"So what do we need to talk about?" Wendell asked. His nerves were still on edge and he opened his humidor to pull out a cigar to calm his anxiety.

"Before I left the jail this morning, the grand jury saw fit to decide that there was a lack of evidence to proceed with bringing Joseph to trial for trying to kill Flannery," Austin replied.

Wendell bit the cap off the cigar and lit the cheroot before speaking. "I can't say that I'm surprised. Joseph carries a lot of weight around here. People are afraid to rock the boat. They know what Joseph is capable of doing – in jail or not. What are your concerns?"

"My concern is that he's going to kill Flannery. We have to help that woman. Joseph Thurgood can't be going around killing everybody that he wants just so he can grab their land. There's been enough bloodshed around here. It needs to stop."

"And how do you propose stopping bloodshed without causing bloodshed?"

Austin bent forward. "I would hope that when word reached Joseph of our involvement, that the show of force would be enough to make him have second thoughts over attacking the widow. If not, then let there be bloodshed in the name of righteousness."

Wendell listened with his mouth open, letting smoke drift out of it. While Austin looked like hell with dark bags under the eyes and a pale complexion, his clarity of thought was something that the father had doubted his son even still possessed. The fly in the ointment was that Wendell didn't agree with Austin's plan. He didn't want to crush his son's newfound conviction, but he had no desire to engage in a battle with the Thurgoods. The standoff with them had been enough to convince him that no one would win that war. "You forget that this is about revenge now instead of just land. I don't think Joseph can be dissuaded."

"Then we fight."

"Austin, I have no wish whatsoever of getting into a feud with Joseph. People will die, and it might be us.

And secondly, I haven't been much better than him when it comes to acquiring land. I may not have killed anyone, but probably only because it never came to that."

"Now is the time to right some of our wrongs then."

Wendell leaned back in his chair and rubbed his forehead. As he contemplated his recent vow to be a better person, he couldn't bring himself to willingly be part of a battle that he had no stake in. "I'm sorry, Austin, but I won't be party to something where we could lose all that we have, including possibly our lives, for someone other than family. Flannery Vogel is not our problem, sad as her life has been. The answer is no."

The resolve in Austin seemed to melt away like a snowman on a sunny day. His shoulders slumped and his face sagged. "Very well, then. I understand completely," he said. He got up and walked out of the house without saying another word.

∞

Boone found himself alone at the ranch. Flannery had taken Jenny and Savannah into Trinidad to do some shopping. With nobody around the place, he didn't know what to do with himself after he finished replacing the broken windows in the house. As much as he was loath to admit it, he'd gotten so accustomed to being with the family all the time that being alone now felt odd. He walked out of the barn and happened to glance over at Jimmy's headstone. At that instant, he knew the time had come to pay his first visit to his friend's grave. He couldn't avoid the gesture any longer.

"Jimmy, I guess I've stayed away from here about as long as I can," Boone said as he squatted next to the tombstone. "If I'd known I'd never get to see you again, I would have made sure to tell you how much you changed my life and made a better man out of me. Hell, you made a man out of me – period. I guess we always think we have more time than we do. I planned to come here for a visit, but just never got around to it. Truth be told, I wouldn't be here now if I hadn't run into some hard times and needed your help. The one thing I can swear to you though is that if I'd had known you'd passed, I would have been here on the double to help Flannery. I certainly owed you that much."

Boone's legs were beginning to ache from the squatting so he plopped down onto his butt, and pulled off his hat.

"That wife of yours is something else. Every once in a while, I can see the girl that you used to brag about as we sat around the campfire, but life has kicked her around pretty good. I think in time she'll get back to being her old self. She's already better than when I first got here. Flannery is a fine woman, and I can see why you fell in love with her. And your daughter brings such joy into this world. You'd be so proud of her. I'm just crazy about Savannah. Sometimes, I think I love her as much as if she were mine own. I've never felt that way about a child in my life, but she is special. Just look at me – I'm smiling just talking about her. I hope you're not mad that I'm so fond of Savannah. I admit it sure isn't fair to you. If I'm being honest, I'm right fond of Flannery, too. She makes me want to be a better man just like you used to do for me. I guess I should put in a word about Jenny while I'm at it. She's my bud . . ."

Boone heard the sound of wagon wheels and jumped up. He started to scurry away from the grave, but realized he was too late. As the family returned home, he stood there looking sheepish while he waited to greet them.

"Just paying my respects," he said.

There was an awkward pause before Jenny said, "There's nothing wrong with that. We all come out here and catch Jimmy up on the news."

Flannery made a weak attempt at a smile. "Jimmy would be proud of you for the way you've looked out for all of us."

Boone made a slight nod of his head before deciding to try to change the subject. "You two don't look very excited after a shopping trip to town."

The women exchanged glances, and Flannery sighed before speaking. "While we were in Trinidad, the sheriff had to release Joseph and his men. The grand jury found insufficient evidence to bring the charges to trial."

Boone felt as if he'd taken a punch to the gut. He reflexively took a deep breath to get some air into his lungs. "I sure didn't see that coming. I don't know what to say."

"Sheriff Stout is fit to be tied. He saw us in town and delivered the news. Thank goodness, we didn't cross paths with Joseph and his men. I don't think I could have stood the sight of them."

"This puts us in a bad spot. We can't sit in that house forever," Boone said.

"I agree. I've been debating with myself all the way home whether Joseph will consider himself lucky to get out of this scrape and leave us alone or if the whole thing will just embolden him."

"It's been my experience that men like Joseph Thurgood don't back down. If anything, he'll think he's above the law now."

"You're probably right. I fear we're all doomed. Maybe I should send Jenny with Savannah back home to my brother's place. They'll be safe and taken care of there. But one way or the other, I'm staying to the end. They can bury me beside Jimmy if it comes to that."

Tears ran down Jenny's cheeks, and she pulled Savannah tightly against her bosom. "Today started out so nice, and now look at it. This beats anything I've ever seen in my entire days."

Boone was growing uncomfortable with the direction the conversation was taking. He uneasily shifted his weight from one foot to the other. Finally, he said, "How is your hand feeling?"

Flannery held up her hand and gazed at the back of it. She had a dark bruise and a forming scab to show for her gallantry. "My hand is a little stiff when I use it, but it's healing just fine. I've known real pain, and this is nothing."

Jenny went from crying to cackling. "She's talking about childbirth," she said between gasps for air. "Old Flannery is the first woman to ever bear the pain of delivering a child – just ask her. I've had to hear about it enough, and I guess you do too now."

Folding her arms, Flannery turned her head and gave Jenny a harsh look. "You're the one that brought it up – not me."

Boone wanted to run to the bunkhouse and hide. If he had his way, Flannery and Jenny would not air such private matters in front of him. "Let's get the wagon unhitched and then we can try to figure out what's the best thing for us to do to be safe." He scurried away toward the barn.

Flannery pulled the wagon up to the barn, and Boone helped her unhitch the team while Jenny whisked Savannah off to the house. The two worked in silence the entire time until the horses were back in their stalls.

"So what do you think about my idea of sending Jenny and Savannah back home?" Flannery asked as she closed a stall door.

Boone rubbed his chin as he studied on the question. "Well, I'm not wild about the idea, though I certainly understand it. I think it will be mighty hard on you without those two here. Shoot, it'll be hard on me. Most days, Savannah is the highlight of it, but I'd never forgive myself if something was to happen to them and I talked you out of sending them away."

Flannery straightened her posture the way she always did when something didn't set well with her. "That wasn't much of an answer at all. You were all over the place. Basically, you're really saying that it's my decision and you'll go along with whatever it is."

Boone smiled. "Well, you are the boss. I just do what I'm told."

"I think we both know that's not true any longer. You have as much say around here as I have, and I'm fine with that. You know what you're doing a whole lot more than I do. I think I'll wait a couple more days before deciding whether to send them away. We can see how things are playing out," Flannery said. She took a quick step toward Boone and kissed him on the cheek. "Thank you for all you've done for us." She dashed out of the barn without another word.

Boone stood there too stunned to even attempt a reply. With his mouth open as if he was trying to catch flies, he lightly touched the spot where she had kissed him. Flannery Vogel had confounded him since the moment he had met her, but nothing felt as confusing as what she had just done. He had no idea what to make of the situation, but he smiled, nonetheless.

Chapter 16

Joseph had sulked around the house on his first day home after being released from jail. He and Emma were barely on speaking terms, and he never even bothered to ask her where she was going when she abruptly left the house shortly after his return. All he wanted out of the day was a bath, shave, and some clean clothes. At supper that night, he never said a word to his wife, but he was so busy shoving the delicious-tasting meal into his mouth that conversation would have been nearly impossible anyway. Jail food gave a man an appetite.

By the next morning at the breakfast table, the simmering feud was just waiting to come to a boil.

"I warned you to leave Flannery Vogel alone," Emma blurted out.

"Woman, just shut up. I'll do what I please. Hunter's death must be revenged," Joseph yelled.

"Don't you dare take that tone with me. I'll say what needs to be said and you'll listen. You could have gotten Elliot killed. Is that what you want – to bury two sons in a little over a week?"

"Better to die fighting for your family than to be a coward like Logan."

"Logan is no such thing. Having a conscience doesn't make him a coward. As much as it grieves me to say this, Hunter died trying to murder Flannery. Logan was not going to be part of such a thing."

Joseph set his cup down so forcefully that coffee spilled onto the linen tablecloth. "He's always been your favorite and you'll make excuses for him until the day you die."

"Logan is the only one of my boys with a lick of reasoning. Hunter and Elliot would follow you off a cliff and never ask why."

"Well, I'll tell you one thing – Logan will never set foot on this ranch again. I'll see to that."

Emma stared at Joseph, trying to remember when she had ever loved the man. A memory came to her of long ago when the boys were all young and the family had spent the day picnicking at the river. The whole family had had a wonderful time. That recollection now seemed like a lifetime ago and somebody else's family. "You'll do no such thing. Yesterday, I went and warned him you were home, but that was only to allow you time to cool down before he comes over here. If you try to keep my son away from me, I will divorce you. I'll take half of everything, and you know it. It was my family's money that got you started in the first place. And another thing, I transferred five thousand dollars into Logan's account and three thousand into Jill's account while you were in jail. They deserve that much. Jill will be able to live on that money, and Logan can start his own ranch or do whatever he wants. You certainly never paid them a fair wage."

Joseph jumped up from the table so violently that he toppled over his chair. "What? You've ruined us. That's almost all the cash we have on hand. How could you? You'll never get away with this," he screamed into his wife's face.

In a cool and detached voice, Emma said, "There is nothing you can do about it now. The deed is done."

"We'll see about that." Joseph grabbed his hat and stomped out of the house.

A few minutes later, Joseph rode out of the barn. He pointed his horse toward town and spurred the animal into a lope. Even as he rushed through the breeze, he felt as if he might suffocate. It seemed as if the empire he'd worked decades to build was crumbling at his feet. Hunter was dead, the sheriff had had the audacity to arrest him, and now his wife had given away a small fortune. He didn't understand how the fates could be so cruel when all he had wanted was to build a legacy for his family. By the time he reached Trinidad, his horse was lathered and had its tongue hanging out of its mouth as it snorted for air. Joseph tied his mount in front of the bank and stormed inside the building. The clerk tried to offer his assistance, but Joseph brushed past him and entered Oscar Hamilton's office.

"You had no right to allow Emma to transfer my money," Joseph bellowed.

The accosting caused Oscar to pull back his head and raise his eyebrows. He had to gather his resolve to overcome his initial fear of being attacked. "Emma's name is on the account, same as yours. I had no legal reason to stop her. You shouldn't have made it a joint account if you didn't want her to have control of your money," he fired back.

"You could have tried talking her out of it."

"I did ask her if she was sure that she wanted to give away that much money, and she insisted that she did."

Joseph kicked the chair sitting in front of the desk. "Damn that woman. If she can transfer it to them, then I can transfer it back."

"No, you can't. It isn't your money any longer. You are out of luck."

"I ought to give you a beating for this."

"You put a hand on me and you'll be dining in the jail again, and that's a promise. Since you're already riled, you might as well know that I can't lend you the money to buy the Cruft place now. You don't have enough collateral."

"This is just great. I don't know what I ever did to deserve all this grief. We should hang every banker in the country," Joseph yelled.

Joseph stormed out of the bank onto the boardwalk. He was ready to mount his horse when he realized he was going to kill the animal if he wasn't careful. He led the gelding to a water trough and let it drink its fill before climbing onto the saddle. With his anger fading into despair, he rode out of town with his horse gaiting at a walk. When he reached the crossroad, he headed toward Logan's home before he actually made the decision to pay his son a visit. The trip took a good hour at the slow pace, and by the time he reached the house, Joseph had drifted into feeling sorry for himself and thinking that the whole world was against him. He found Logan in the yard, swinging an axe in a rhythm that a couple could have danced to as he split firewood.

"Good to see you haven't hired help to do the chores since your newfound wealth," Joseph said from atop the saddle.

Logan stopped his work and rested the axe against his leg. "I didn't ask for it. In fact, I didn't know anything about it until it had already happened."

"There's nothing stopping you from giving the money back."

"While that's factually true, Momma would be furious with me and you would be elated. We both know where my loyalties lie. So, no, I'm not giving you your money back. I guess you can consider it the cost of having me out of your hair."

"What are you going to do with the money?" Joseph asked in a voice that sounded even nonchalant to his own ears.

"Don't know yet. I may start my own ranch or I may move away. I'm changing my mind like the wind right now."

The answer stirred the ire in Joseph. He straightened his posture and squeezed the reins in a death grip. "You never did know what you wanted in life. Weak is what you are. You might have gotten the brains of the bunch, but you have no heart. I'll never forgive you for not going into battle with us."

Logan looked up at his father and studied him. His pa looked old for his age as if all his efforts to build his empire had come at a heavy toll and sapped his vitality. Logan felt detached like he was looking at a stranger. The last couple of weeks had drained away his loyalty and his spirit to the point that he mostly felt numb. "I've never murdered anyone and I don't plan to start now. I'm sure Hank and Jose feel real appreciated from their unmarked graves for their loyalty to you for all those years of work."

"You've never wanted anything bad enough then. This world is divided into winners and losers. I guess we know what you are. And Hank and Jose were paid for their work." The disdain in Joseph's voice sounded palpable.

"Maybe I'll want the Cruft place bad enough to bid against you for it."

Joseph's face turned red, and he climbed off his horse. "I can't even bid on it now that your mother ruined our finances. I'll show you how bad I wanted it."

"You take one more step toward me and I'll make you sorry," Logan warned as he tossed the axe to the side.

Joseph kept on charging forward. Logan, instead of leading with his dominant hand, threw a left hook. The punch caught his pa completely by surprise as it smashed into his jaw. The blow dropped him to his knees. As he swayed there, looking stunned, Logan came down with a vicious right to the face. Joseph toppled over in a heap with his left cheek split open.

"I warned you to stop. When did you ever listen? When? The good old days when you could do whatever you wanted and get by with it are now gone. You just can't see it. You're blind to progress," Logan yelled. He turned his back and stalked toward his house.

Joseph rolled onto his back and pulled out his revolver. As he twisted his body toward his son, he hollered, "I'll kill you, you little bastard."

Logan turned around to face his nemesis. "Go ahead. I already feel dead inside. So come on."

Joseph took aim at his son. His hand began to shake before he dropped again onto his back.

With a shake of his head, Logan resumed his journey and disappeared into his house. From a window, he watched his father. Joseph rested on the ground for a few minutes and then got to his feet. He stumbled to his horse and rode away.

"It's a proud day to be a Thurgood," Logan whispered.

Chapter 17

The moping behavior of Flannery had caught the watchful eye of Jenny. Ever since the news of Joseph Thurgood's release from jail, the old black woman had noticed the change in behavior. Flannery wasn't her normal take-charge self and hardly engaged Jenny in conversations. In fact, Jenny worried that Flannery looked tired and sickly.

While Savannah napped, and Boone worked out in the barn, Jenny decided the time had come for a talk. "What's wrong? Is this Joseph Thurgood business about to get the best of you?" she asked.

"Yes, of course, it is. I don't know how we can continue to defend ourselves. And I'm tortured trying to decide if I should send you and Savannah away for safety's sake," Flannery said. She dropped into a chair at the kitchen table with a thud.

Jenny sat down across from her. "I won't give you an argument either way. I don't want to leave you, but I couldn't bear something happening to our baby, either. I'll do whatever you think is best, but if we go, I'm liable to lose my mind worrying about you."

"I know you would," Flannery said. She reached across the table and placed her palm on top of Jenny's hand.

"Life shouldn't be this hard."

"I agree with that. If I wasn't so hardheaded, I would just sell this place and get on with my life, but I just can't make myself do that. Jimmy is buried here, after all."

"There's nothing wrong with sticking to your principles."

"And there's something else . . ."

Wrinkling her nose, Jenny asked, "Oh, and what might that be?"

Flannery glanced up from the table and looked Jenny straight in the eyes as she squeezed her friend's hand. "The other day when we got back from town, Boone and I were talking in the barn. I felt so overwhelmed from the news, and so thankful that we had him with us that I kissed him on the cheek. As soon as I did it, I was embarrassed to death. I skedaddled out of there so quickly your head would spin. I've had a hard time looking at him ever since then."

Jenny's eyes got as big as silver dollars. She prided herself in knowing Flannery's state of mind, and for picking up on emotions of others, but this news caught her totally off guard. "I thought you two was acting rather queer around each other. My, my, my. You fooled old Jenny. I didn't see that one coming. So why do you think you kissed him?"

"Jenny, I don't know. I just acted on impulse, I guess."

"Do you think you're developing feelings for Boone?"

"He was Jimmy's friend. Even if it was true, and I'm not saying that it is, it would be so wrong. I'm a widow with a daughter. I shudder to think what people would say."

Jenny let out one of her belly laughs that shook her whole body. "That's right, you are a widow. That means you're the one still alive. Jimmy has been gone for two years. Instead of me sitting here giggling, I'd be crying if I thought a young thing like you was going to spend the rest of her days alone. I'm old and I won't be here forever. I'll go to my grave a smidgen easier knowing you have someone looking after you and loving you."

"Do you really think I'll marry again?"

"You'd best if you don't want me rolling around in my grave for eternity."

"I just never imagined me ever doing such a thing again."

"Well, you need to start imagining it. It ain't natural for people to be alone. Shoot, I would have lost my mind a long time ago if I didn't have you and now Savannah in my life."

"You are so sweet, and I don't know what I would do without you. I love you just like my mother."

"I love you, too. So now the big question – are you getting smitten with Boone?"

Flannery turned red and she could feel her ears burning. She resisted the urge to bolt from the table. "I don't know. I've certainly come to change my opinion about him. He's surely has a way about him, and if Savannah is any judge of character, he's a fine man."

The sound of Jenny's laughter again filled the room. She pounded her fist on the table in delight, and even snorted as she tried to catch her breath. When Jenny could finally speak, she said, "Yes, Flannery, we trust Savannah's judgement so soundly that we let her make all the decisions around here."

Jumping up from her seat, Flannery exclaimed, "Honestly, Jenny, you are incorrigible. I think I'll check on Savannah. You've probably awakened her with a fright with all your cackling."

"You just do that. Why don't you ask her to decide about sending us away while you are at it?" Jenny said and started laughing again. "I have to go get clothes in off the line."

As Flannery scurried toward the bedroom, Jenny headed outside, but instead of going to the clothesline, she marched to the barn and found Boone brushing a horse.

"Are you going stir-crazy?" Jenny asked to get Boone's attention.

Boone looked up and smiled. "Yeah, I guess I am. I'm not used to all this idleness. There are so many things that need to be done around here and now we can't get away from the house for fear of getting killed. Something is going to have to give, one way or the other."

"I know it is." Jenny walked over and rubbed the horse's nose. "I think we're all getting a little crazy. I know I'll be glad when this is all over. I just have to believe that God will let the righteous win this one. Lord knows that Flannery has been through enough."

Boone resumed the brushing. "That she has. I guess the not knowing is what gets on my nerves. That Thurgood bunch has all the advantages. If we had a crew, I'd take the fight to them."

"I know you would. You proved your bravery to me. Is there anything else bothering you?"

Boone looked up at Jenny and studied her as he tried to decipher what to make of her question. The woman showed a poker face that gave no hint to the hand she played. He let out a sigh, deciding not to try to be cagey with a woman too smart for deception to work anyway. "She told you, didn't she?" he asked.

Jenny's emotionless face broke into a smile. "She did. What do you think about it?"

"Jenny, I don't have a clue as what to make of it. To tell you truth, that kiss has kept me up the last two nights trying to figure it out. Most of the time, Flannery is so prim and proper, even distant, and then she goes and does that. I'm surprised you didn't end up burying me beside Jimmy just from the shock it gave me."

Folding her arms and nodding her head, Jenny said, "All right, Boone, I get that you were surprised, now I want to know what you thought about it."

Boone flashed an impish grin. "Well, it wasn't the worst thing that has ever happened to me," he said, prompting Jenny to let out an annoyed sounding sigh. "All right, I was flattered, and I wondered if there was a chance we might have a future together. I'd certainly never entertained that notion before that moment. Flannery, at her best, is a fine woman."

"I have to admit that I felt as surprised by the news as you must have been upon receiving the kiss. I usually know Flannery's mind before she does."

"So what do you make of the situation?"

Jenny unfolded her arms and rubbed her chin as she contemplated the question. "Right now, Flannery hasn't decided for sure what it means, but you have certainly wiggled your way into her mind. As hardheaded as that girl is, she may keep you at arm's length for the rest of your days together or you just might be the one to thaw that icy wall she's built up around herself. There's definitely some melting going on."

"And what do you think about it?" Boone asked.

"I'd be as happy as a dog with a bone. I never got my hopes up over such a thing because I know how she is, but you've stirred some feelings that she thought was dead. Savannah being in love with you hasn't hurt any either. Old Jenny might get to raise some more babies around here yet."

Boone turned red and looked down at the horse. "I don't know about that. And I didn't do anything to deserve Savannah's attention. She just chose me anyway."

Jenny let out a laugh and slapped her thighs. "You just keep on being yourself. Babies don't choose to like you because of your clothes or money. They just know what makes them happy. We'll just have to see what happens, but you caused Flannery to get an itch, and an itch usually gets scratched."

The two were laughing when Flannery walked into the barn carrying Savannah.

"You two sure seemed amused. What's so funny?" Flannery asked in a jaded tone.

Jenny gave a warm smile. "We were just discussing Savannah's love of riding with Boone. I told him he was going to make that poor child bowlegged."

Flannery looked at them skeptically and cut her eyes at Jenny. "I thought you were going to get the clothes off the line."

"I'm going to. I just thought I'd check on Boone first. Honestly, Flannery, don't be such a prig. I can run things around here just fine without you needing to tell me what to do. I think you forget who was the one that changed your diapers way back when."

Flannery let out a huff. "I don't think that comment was necessary, but I'm sorry I was brusque. I'll help you with the clothes."

"Let's get at it then. Those clothes must be worrying you something fierce."

Ignoring Jenny, Flannery said, "Boone, I know I spoil this child, but as soon as she woke up, she said she wanted her Boone. Can you watch her long enough to satisfy her?"

"Sure, put her on the horse while I finish brushing it."

"She's too little. She'll fall off."

"Flannery, I'll hold on to her. The last thing in the world I would do is let something happen to that child."

"I guess I should trust you by now. Being overly protective just comes naturally to me." Flannery set her daughter on the horse and walked out of the barn with Jenny.

Boone grasped Savannah around the ankle and then ducked in front of the horse's chest. He popped up on either side of the animal's neck and made faces at the Savannah until the child giggled hysterically.

"You funny," Savannah said.

"No, you're funny."

"You funny, Boone."

"Maybe we're both funny."

"I love you, Boone."

Savannah's words of endearment hit Boone like a punch in the stomach and caught him unprepared. He was overcome with emotions that until recently he never knew he even possessed. His eyes welled with tears and he looked away for a moment. As he moved to the child, he said, "I love you, too." He kissed Savannah on the forehead and hugged her. In all his days, he'd never felt anything remotely close to the bond he felt toward the little girl.

Chapter 18

Any hope Wendell had held that Austin's lucid behavior would continue was quickly dashed when his son returned to the bottle. Austin would only speak to his father when absolutely necessary, and spent most of his time riding around the property in a drunken stupor. He made no pretense of helping around the ranch, leaving the work to Calvin and the ranch hands.

Wendell sat at the table eating a breakfast of ham and eggs while worrying about his son when Austin dragged into the room. Austin shielded his eyes from the bright morning light as he made his way to the table. He dropped into a chair so forcefully that the jolt only added to the pain in his aching head, causing him to wince.

"Only coffee for me," Austin said to the cook.

"You look like hell. You're going to kill yourself if this doesn't stop," Wendell lectured.

"What difference does it make at this point? We're all going to die cowards anyway. Everyone in the county is going to sit around and watch Joseph Thurgood kill Flannery Vogel."

"You barely know the woman. I don't see why this is so important to you. We have enough problems of our own to deal with without taking on hers, too."

The cook brought Austin his coffee and then quickly disappeared from the room.

"We've done a lot of shameful things on this ranch. Things that I was willingly a part of doing. I remember us running a poor family with little children off our land that were merely making camp for the night and would have been gone the next day. We humiliated that father in front of his kids. What would it have hurt to let them stay? I guess I'd like to right some wrongs. That war might have been the ruin of me, but I was a good soldier. I never once shirked my duty, and I was brave, too. I knew we were fighting for a greater good. Maybe I'd just like to feel that way one more time before I die."

Wendell sipped his coffee as he studied over his son's words. "Even if we wanted to help, I don't see how it would be possible. We can't just camp over at the Vogel place and wait for Joseph to come and attack again. We have a ranch to run. Something you surely are shirking out on these days."

If the comment was supposed to make Austin feel guilty, it failed miserably. He just didn't care enough anymore whether he helped out on the ranch or what anyone thought about his behavior. "We'd take the fight to Joseph. That's how we'd do it."

Nodding his head, Wendell said, "I see. In other words, start a range war that could last a long time and get a bunch of people killed."

"Not a war – a battle. I know how to fight. We'd put a stop to all of this in one day."

"I wish I had your confidence in us succeeding in such a scrape, but even if we did, the sheriff might take a dim view of such a thing. That's really not much different from what Joseph is trying to do to Flannery."

"I wouldn't just attack. I'd draw Joseph into a fight. You know what a hothead he is. It wouldn't take anything to start the bullets flying."

Wendell glanced over at his son, realizing how much thought Austin had put into his plan. He was amazed his son had the clarity to even strategize a plan of battle.

Still, Wendell had seen range wars before, and the Davids of the world did not always win against the Goliaths. "I'm sorry, Austin, but I've worked too hard to build this ranch for me to chance losing our lives and all we've worked for to help somebody we barely know. I just won't do it." He expected an outburst from his son, but Austin just nodded his head and seemed resigned to failing to get his way.

"I expected as much. Evil will eventually trump all the good in this world. It's just a matter of time," Austin said.

Wendell had no idea how to respond to his son so he decided to change the subject. "Today is the auction of the Cruft property. Why don't you ride to town with me? I'm going to do my best to keep that ranch out of Joseph's hands. I plan to do my damnedest to keep him from being rewarded for killing Simon."

Austin leaned back in his chair and tilted his head toward the ceiling. As he loudly blew out his breath, he wiped his brow with a shaking hand. "I think I will go. Seeing Joseph lose out on the land would be a small victory. I guess I better eat some breakfast."

After Austin finished his meal, Wendell, Calvin, and he rode into Trinidad to the courthouse. A large crowd had already gathered around the building as they waited for the auctioneer to climb the stairs and begin the sale from the vantage point. The men tied their horses and moved in amongst the gatherers.

Wendell spotted Joseph standing with Elliot and his ranch hands. He noticed that Fred Coup and Milton Frank were standing with the Thurgoods, too. It appeared as if Joseph had hired the men away from other area ranchers. Both men had fought in the war, and had a reputation of being good with guns and of having no qualms about using them when needed. Wendell also spied Logan standing off by himself. He decided to have a word with him.

"You look as if you've lost your last friend," Wendell said when he walked up to Logan.

Logan let out a little grunt. "You could say that. I doubt my old man or Elliot will ever speak to me again."

"You're still family. That tends to allow for a lot of ill will to heal in time."

"See that cut and bruise on Pa's cheek? I put that there. He hates me for not supporting him."

Wendell gazed at the nasty wound on Joseph's face. "Logan, sometimes doing the right thing overrules loyalty. I commend you for having no part in trying to kill Flannery."

Logan grimaced, but didn't make a comment. Selling out his family was one line that he would not cross.

"So are you here to bid on the Cruft ranch?" Wendell asked to change the subject.

"You know, that's what I came here to do just to spite the old man, but standing here, I've come to realize that my heart just isn't into ranching. I think I'm going to take the train back East and see how the civilized folks live. I just might go to college. That's what I always wanted to do."

Wendell patted Logan on the shoulder. "You're still a young man and still have time to find your calling. Life is too short to spend it doing something you hate. Me, I always loved ranching, but I'm not you. Good luck."

"Thank you, Wendell. I wish our families could have gotten along better instead of being so competitive."

"I'm as much to blame for that as Joseph is. The older I get, the sillier it all seems, but it's too late to stop now."

The auctioneer climbed the steps and started making the announcements for the auction. By the time the bidding began, Wendell had returned to stand with Austin and Calvin.

Theodore Hanks was the first rancher to make an offer. He was quickly outbid by Roger Hart. As the two men competed for the property, Wendell glanced over at Joseph, surprised by the rancher's lack of bidding. Joseph shot him a glare that looked lethal. Wendell grinned at him and raised his hand to bid.

The three ranchers bandied back and forth in their quest to own the Cruft ranch until Wendell raised his bid to ten thousand dollars. His bold move silenced the other two men.

The auctioneer hollered, "Going once, going twice, sold to Wendell Starr." He pounded his gavel once and smiled at the thought of his hefty commission.

As the crowd dispersed, Joseph stalked toward Wendell like a train on a long downhill run.

"Well, aren't you just so proud of yourself? I did all the work and you're the one that ends up with the Cruft ranch," Joseph fumed.

"Are you confessing to murdering Simon?" Wendell asked in a calm voice.

Elliot and the ranch hands crowded around Wendell, Calvin, and Austin in an intimidating show of force.

"I never said any such thing. Don't go putting words into my mouth."

"You were free to bid just like everyone else. I was surprised to see that you didn't."

"I had my reasons and they're none of your business."

Wendell was struck by the absurdity of Joseph being riled that he lost out on the land when he never even attempted to purchase the property. "If you didn't want it, why in the hell are you mad at me? Talk about stupidity," he yelled.

"You want to talk about stupidity, I'll show it to you," Joseph screamed as he pecked Austin on the chest. "This half-wit son of yours is the sorriest excuse for a human I've ever met. He comes back from the war crazier than an Injun on peyote just because he had to kill some people in battle. Poor little sissy."

Logan came running toward the men in hopes of getting in between the two families before there was bloodshed. Just as he neared the group, a shot rang out.

"That's enough right now unless you want to revisit my jail," Sheriff Stout barked.

Joseph turned to face the sheriff, his face red and livid with anger. He bared his teeth and focused a menacing stare at the lawman. "Why don't you mind your own business," he screamed.

"This is my business. Keep it up and I'll throw your ass in jail for disorderly conduct."

Joseph opened his mouth and then thought better of it.

"Smart move. Now go home," the sheriff ordered.

Joseph jerked his head around to see Wendell. "Someday you'll get what's coming to you," he warned. He stomped off toward Logan.

Logan turned and started walking toward his horse in hopes of evading another confrontation. As he tried to escape, he cringed at the sound of the footsteps of his father jogging his way.

"I bet you're just tickled to death that Wendell bought that land out from under me because your mother ruined our finances," Joseph accused.

Logan stopped and let out a sigh that caused his shoulders to sag. As he turned to face his father, he felt like a man that had grown old before his time. "You know, Pa, I just don't care anymore. I'm done with all of it. Please just leave me alone."

"You're a traitor to your family and a disgrace to your name. I always knew you weren't tough enough for this world, but I never thought you'd turn your back on us. Hunter must be rolling over in his grave."

"You can call it avenging Hunter's death, but I'll just call it what it is – murder."

Joseph leaned in so that his face nearly touched Logan's ear. "I'll tell you one thing – I'll have Flannery Vogel's land before it's all said and done. After I sell some beef to get some money again, she's as good as dead. It's taken longer than I planned, but I'll get there – count on it. I thought when Hunter and I killed Jimmy, she would sell the place first thing, but I was wrong about that." He smiled, proud of his revelation.

Logan's mouth dropped open and he looked up toward the heavens. Though he'd initially suspected his father and Hunter as the culprits in the murder, he'd accepted his father's word that the family had no hand in Jimmy Vogel's death. The news disgusted him and made him ashamed to be a Thurgood. "You lied to me, and you made that poor woman a widow just so you could get her land. You don't even see the irony in that they killed Hunter in self-defense, when by your book, they were entitled to kill him for revenge, but yet you think you have the right to kill her. You make the means justify the end just so you can get the land. That's all that really matters to you. It doesn't have a thing to do with Hunter."

"You can see it any way that you like. In the end, Elliot will thank me when I leave my empire to him while you'll probably end up being a clerk in a general store. There'll come a day when you rue ever turning your back on your family. I'll never speak to or of you again," Joseph said before turning and walking away.

Logan stood there, watching his father join Elliot and the hired hands. He felt like a man without a country, but he held no doubts that he'd done the right thing. All through his life, he'd considered himself loyal to his family even to the point of doing some questionable deeds, but he drew the line at murder. As he turned toward his horse, he wondered whether he even had a purpose in life, and if he did, what in the hell it might be.

Chapter 19

As Boone pounded the last nail into the board to complete the fence, he said, "I think Jimmy would be proud of us. We surely have come close to expanding the corral as he must have envisioned it."

Flannery straightened up to a standing position from her squat, and clapped her hands together to knock the dust off them. "Oh, I'm certain he would be. I think we did a fine job if I do say so myself. Thank you for all your hard work. I know I couldn't have done it without you," she said.

"Now, if we can ever just get back to working this ranch so we have something to put in this corral. I tell you, Flannery, I don't know what to do next." Boone stood and tossed the hammer to the ground.

"Maybe we're at the point where we need to get back to normal around here, and if we have trouble, we'll just deal with it. I've had about all of this I can take. I'm ready to get back to ranching."

Boone smiled and made a quick nod of his head. "That's my girl. That's just what I wanted to hear. I thought . . ." Boone began blushing, and stumbled to speak again. "I didn't mean anything by that – honest. It just kind of came out."

Flannery rubbed her forehead as she tried to decide how to respond. "Boone, this is my fault. I didn't mean to mislead you with that kiss the other day. Just like with you now, it just kind of happened without thought. Maybe it's from all the stress we're living under."

Looking embarrassed, Boone waved his hand through the air as if the whole thing was just a little misunderstanding. "You don't have to explain yourself to me. I understand completely. Heck, I think it's a miracle that we're even friends."

With a pained smile, Flannery nodded her head. "We are friends – maybe even good friends."

The couple stood there looking at each other. Neither of them could seem to think of anything else to say and the silence grew uncomfortable. Flannery licked her lips in a nervous habit she had developed in her youth. Boone could feel his heart racing in his chest, and sweat running down his sides. He fought the urge to bolt for the barn, but instead, in a moment where emotions triumphed over logic, he leaned over and kissed Flannery on the lips. Expecting to get shoved away, Boone braced himself and nearly lost his balance when Flannery threw her arms around his neck and pulled him into her. They became oblivious to the world around them as they lost themselves in their pent-up desires.

Jenny had been standing at the window, washing dishes and watching Boone and Flannery. She had grown alarmed when the couple had stood there staring at each other, fearing they were on the verge of a knock-down drag-out. She had contemplated rushing outside to divert their attention, but when they kissed instead, she let out a squeal that startled Savannah and caused the child to flinch. "I think Boone is going to be your new daddy," she hollered. She took Savannah by the hands and began waltzing around the room while humming a melody.

As they danced, Jenny glanced out a front window and saw a rider approaching. She scooped up Savannah and ran out onto the front porch. "There's a rider coming," she bellowed.

Boone and Flannery came barreling around the corner of the house with rifles in hand. As far Jenny could tell, the impending visitor must have cooled whatever passions had been flowing between them because neither seemed the least bit self-conscious.

"I think it is Logan again," Jenny announced.

Once Logan was close enough to be identified for sure, Boone and Flannery set their guns up against the porch rail and waited.

"Logan, good to see you again," Flannery greeted.

"Good to see you, too," Logan responded.

"I'm glad to have the chance to thank you for your warning. You surely saved our lives. We'll be indebted to you forever."

"I'm glad I could be of some help. It really is the least I could do. I hate it that Hank and Jose got killed, but I do understand the situation."

"It kind of comes with the territory when you attack us," Boone interjected.

"Oh, I know it does. I just regret they died for my pa's foolish actions."

"What brings you out here this time?" Flannery asked.

Logan climbed down from his horse and dropped the reins. "I'm going to be going away and wanted to make you aware of what I know. Just because my father was lucky enough to get by with what he did one time, he's not going to be grateful for his good fortune and give up. He'll be coming again. Right now, he's low on funds and couldn't buy this place if something were to happen to you folks. His plan, as of now, is to wait until he's sold some cattle and then come for you. So I'm guessing you may be safe until the fall."

With a sigh of relief, Flannery said, "That is somewhat good news. The waiting is almost unbearable."

"I'm sure it is. I need to tell you something else, but I want you to understand something first. I seriously doubt my father and I will ever speak again, but at the end of the day, he's still my father, and I would never testify against him. So what I'm about to tell you, I would deny if you ever tried to attribute it to me, but I believe you are entitled to the truth about your husband," Logan said and then hesitated as he worked up his nerve to continue. "I had their word that they had no part in it, but I now believe that Pa and Hunter killed Jimmy – I'm so sorry."

Flannery began to tremble, and covered her face with her hands. Jenny, seeing Flannery in so much pain, threw her arm around her friend and pulled her into an embrace.

"Are you sure?" Boone asked.

"Unless Pa told me just to rile me, I would say it's true," Logan replied.

Boone closed his eyes and squeezed his lips firmly together. His face turned red and he balled his hands in fists so tightly that his knuckles turned white. "I don't know why I'm shocked," he mumbled.

"I'm truly sorry for all the pain my family has inflicted upon you, and I hope things work out for you all. I best be going. If I never see you again, know that I'll be thinking of you." Logan turned and grabbed his horse's dangling reins.

Flannery reached out and put her hand on Logan's arm. "Thank you for coming and telling us the truth.

I'm beholden to you. Godspeed on your journey. I wish you the best."

Logan grimly nodded his head before mounting his horse. He rode away without saying another word.

As soon as Logan was out of sight, Boone started cussing up a storm and mumbling to himself. Jenny rushed Savannah into the house as Boone stomped around the yard like a madman.

"Boone, calm yourself before you have a stroke," Flannery pleaded. "I'm not sure why you're getting all worked up just because we know the killer. Jimmy is just as dead now as he was yesterday. That is the part that hasn't changed and matters the most."

Boone paused in his pacing and turned toward Flannery. "I suppose you have a point, but now we know the murderers for sure. I'm going to kill Joseph Thurgood if it's the last thing I ever do."

"You can't just go over there and murder him. You'd either get yourself killed or hanged for it. You need to remember that we need you around here. Savannah has had a hard enough start to life and doesn't need you yanked out of it."

Boone managed a weak smile. He liked the sound of hearing that he was needed. "Yeah, you're right. I for sure want to be around for Savannah, but I will kill him."

"And another thing – I better not hear talk like that in front of my daughter again. You'll have her talking like a ranch hand if that continues. I will not tolerate such behavior from you or her."

With an embarrassed sounding laugh, Boone said, "Yes, ma'am."

"Now that we have some freedom to move around the place, let's go check on the herd. I'll tell Jenny our plans if you'll go get the horses ready."

After the horses were saddled, Boone and Flannery set out in search of the cattle herd. As they rode, neither of them had much to say and spent most of their time staring off at the mountains in the distance. The conversation never turned more serious than a mention of some new prairie dog holes that had been dug since their last outing.

Flannery's mind raced over the details of what had happened out by the corral. She had never dreamed that the reticent Boone would kiss her, and she was truly astounded by her own reaction to what had happened. Never in a million years would she have thought that she would so ardently return the kiss. A part of her felt guilty for kissing another man after the death of her husband, but a little voice in her head that she wasn't quite ready to acknowledge told her that there was a lot more to what had happened than just a lonely woman needing a little attention.

Now that Boone had calmed down from his outburst over learning that Joseph had killed Jimmy, he had a hard time even looking at Flannery. He still couldn't believe he'd found the courage to kiss her. Women had never been his strong suit. Jimmy had used to tease him unmercifully about his clumsiness around the female persuasion. Boone wondered what Jimmy would think if he knew his friend had finally found his courage with Jimmy's widow. And Jenny's talk with him about Flannery notwithstanding, he still couldn't fathom how as fine of a woman as Flannery would have so willingly kissed the likes of him. He just didn't know what to think.

They found the herd grazing in a lush valley with a creek running through its center. The cattle and yearlings looked healthy from feeding on the tall grass, and the calves were growing rapidly on a plentiful milk supply. After discussing the state of the herd, they headed for home without ever mentioning the kissing.

Jenny was placing the plates on the table for supper when Boone and Flannery entered the home. She smiled at them. "You two go wash up. The meal will be ready by the time you finish," she said.

As the food was being passed around the table, Savannah said, "Boone is going to be my daddy."

Boone turned about three shades of red, and stared down at his plate. He wanted to crawl under the table and die on the spot.

Flannery cut her eyes at Jenny. The black woman smiled back at her as innocently as a lamb.

"And where did you hear that?" Flannery asked.

"Jenny," Savannah answered.

Jenny tugged the plate of biscuits away from Flannery. "Don't you go blaming me. There is a barn with some privacy to it if you two didn't want the whole world to see you. I was doing the dishes and you were right there in front of my eyeballs. I might be old, but I'm not blind. All I did was just get a little excited and say what I was thinking."

"Well, the next time I'll make sure we're out of sight of prying eyes – that's for sure," Flannery said.

"Good to know that there will be a next time," Jenny responded with a devilish grin.

"Honestly, Jenny, some of the things that come out of that mouth."

Boone couldn't make eye contact with anyone. He ate his meal while staring at his food, and never said a single word throughout the meal.

Much to her own surprise, Flannery felt emboldened by getting caught. To her way of thinking, things were out in the open now, wherever it might lead. While Boone looked as if he might crawl away and die somewhere, she wasn't worried that he wouldn't come back around if that's where things were headed. Men weren't horses. You could lead them to water and get them to drink their fill when it came to loving. And as for Jenny, she knew her too well to be embarrassed by her antics. With the news that Joseph wouldn't be attacking them any time soon, she felt better than she had in a long time.

When Boone finished eating, he said, "Now that we know we're safe, I'm moving back to the bunkhouse so I won't be underfoot all the time. You ladies have a nice evening."

Jenny grinned mischievously. "Maybe if you're real good, Flannery will come tuck you in at bedtime."

The comment caused Boone to bolt for the door. As he made his exit, he could hear the old black woman cackling and pounding the table.

Chapter 20

Two days after the auction, Joseph continued to rant over its outcome to any of the ranch hands that had the misfortune to get cornered by him. He was irked to no end by the notion that the land he had coveted had been purchased by Wendell, and his treatment at the hands of Sheriff Stout only served to add humiliation into the volatile mix of emotions.

Joseph gathered Elliot and the ranch hands together in the barn just before quitting time. "I want everybody ready to ride at nine o'clock tonight. I'm not ready to go kill all the people that need a good killing just yet, but I thought we'd pay Flannery and Wendell a little visit to do some target practice on their cattle to let them know that I'm thinking about them," he said with a smirk.

Elliot looked at the ranch hands to see if any might object to the plan. He quickly realized that it would fall upon him to be a voice of reason. "Pa, aren't you worried about starting a war with Wendell? I can understand going after the widow, but Wendell can match us man for man and then some."

The question only seemed to further enflame Joseph's ill mood. He pursed his lips and stared at Elliot until his son cast his eyes to the ground. "Now you're beginning to sound like Logan. Another useless son is all I need around here. Wendell is all bark and no bite. I'm not worried about him at all. And Calvin is too worried about inheriting the ranch to ever risk his own life. We all know that Austin is just plain crazy. He's more apt to kill himself than one of us. I don't want to hear any more such talk. Do I make myself clear?"

Elliot meekly nodded his head.

"We can get to both ranches by riding the river's edge so we don't have to worry about tracks. Not that I'm worried anyway. If a grand jury won't hold me responsible for trying to kill Flannery, they sure in the hell aren't going to bother with some dead cattle. Any questions?"

While none of the men looked thrilled with the assignment, they shook their heads before departing for the bunkhouse to fix supper.

The rancher returned to the barn at nine o'clock sharp, and found the horses saddled, including his own mount. Joseph couldn't help but notice the surly mood of his crew. All the men were bundled up in jackets and chaps for the cool evening ride, and looked as if they would prefer to be anywhere else. "Let's ride," he said.

Joseph led the men to the river where they all rode into the water's edge and headed toward Wendell's ranch. With the moon a few days past full and the night cloudless with a blanket of stars, the men had sufficient light in which to see for easy travel. The thrill of putting his plan into action had greatly improved Joseph's mood, and as they rode, he tried with little success to lighten the mood of the crew with stories of his past deeds. He finally gave up and continued on in silence. When he recognized an outcrop of rocks, he knew he'd crossed onto Wendell's property.

"Let's go find us some cattle. Keep your ears open," Joseph instructed.

The men fanned out and began their search for one of Wendell's herds. The land consisted of rolling hills, swales, and valleys, and provided plenty of places for the cattle to bed. Nearly an hour passed before the soft mooing of a cow off in the distance drifted their way. Joseph put his horse into a trot and headed in the direction of the sound. A few minutes later, he caught sight of the herd.

"Spread out a little and get your rifles ready," Joseph ordered. "Fire off as many rounds as you can."

The seven men stretched out in a line to where they were about ten yards apart from one another. When the last man took his position, Joseph pulled his Winchester from the scabbard and took aim. He fired the first shot, ending the stillness of the night. The men let loose with a volley that sounded as if a war had suddenly erupted. By the second barrage of gunfire, the herd stampeded away from the loud mayhem.

"Let's go run them to death," Elliot suggested.

"No, we don't want to overstay our welcome," Joseph said and chuckled. "We've accomplished our goal. Let's get the hell out of here."

Joseph put his horse into a lope in the direction from which they had come. When the men reached the Purgatoire River, they steered their mounts into the water and headed in the direction of the Vogel spread. The traveling took well over an hour before reaching the ranch as they followed the winding stream. Another two hours passed before they finally found Flannery's herd in the valley where she and Boone had last checked on them. By that time, the men were getting tired and had begun to grumble amongst themselves. Once again, they opened fire on the cattle, causing another stampede.

The roar of the gunshots carried a great distance in the still night. Boone had stepped out of the bunkhouse to relieve himself when the sound of the salvo reached him. He ran inside to grab his rifle and then sprinted barefoot to the barn. With no time to waste, he pulled his horse from the stall, slipped on its bridle, and then rode away on bareback at a gallop. The gunfire stopped as suddenly as it had begun, but Boone guided the horse toward the herd, thinking the shots had come from that vicinity. Back in the day, he'd spent a good amount of time riding without a saddle, and easily kept his balance as the horse negotiated the terrain through dips and around obstacles. As he topped a hill, he saw the riders headed toward the river. Their distance from him made attempting to take aim in the dark nearly impossible, but he tried nonetheless. The marauders took off at a run at the sound of the first shot while Boone continued firing until he'd emptied his rifle. With no more bullets, he could only watch as the men disappeared over a ridge.

"This isn't going to end until Joseph Thurgood is dead," Boone muttered.

He rode down into the valley and spotted the shapes of dead cattle. The rest of the herd was nowhere in sight. He had no desire to attempt to get a count of the dead animals in the dark, so he turned his horse for home. Well before he reached the house, he could see the glow of lit lamps, dashing his hope of waiting to break the news until morning. Flannery and Jenny were standing on the porch waiting for him.

"What happened?" Flannery asked in a voice so meek that Boone could barely hear her.

"Somebody attacked the herd. I'm sure it was Joseph. I don't know how many head are dead, and the herd has run to who knows where," Boone answered solemnly.

"Damn it to hell," Flannery cursed and began crying. "I don't know how much more of this I can take."

Jenny put her hand on Flannery's arm. "Don't go getting yourself all riled up. We're all still alive and healthy. We still have that to be thankful for," she said.

Boone slid off the horse and climbed the stairs. Having endured such a dire evening, he no longer cared what anyone thought about his feelings for Flannery. He took her in his arms and patted her back. "There's nothing we can do until morning, and we all need to get some rest. Everything is going to be fine."

"No, it won't. We're all going to die," Flannery blubbered into his chest.

"I'm going to take care of all this. I know I've waited too long, but that ends as of now. Sometimes you have to take the fight to the enemy, no matter what the odds. We're going to be just fine – you have my word."

Chapter 21

Before the break of dawn, Boone had flung himself out of bed. He'd barely slept after the ordeal the previous night anyway, and as he moved around the bunkhouse, his limbs felt like they had minds of their own and he yawned constantly. With nothing else to do, he went to the barn to feed the horses and milk the cow. When he finished the chores and walked outside, he saw that a light was on in the house. Flannery greeted him at the door and took the pail of milk from him to set on the table.

"Thank you. I don't know that I have the strength to milk today. I didn't sleep a wink after you got back last night. I hate to say this, but you look as bad as I feel," Flannery said. She dropped into a chair with her shoulders slumped.

Boone smiled. "So much for flattery," he said before inhaling deeply. "Thank goodness, Jenny still has the strength to cook. That bacon smells wonderful."

Jenny turned away from the stove. "It's a good thing somebody still knows how to make breakfast around here. Flannery must think she's a woman of leisure. She just wants to sit around the kitchen so that she can whine and feel sorry for herself."

Flannery cast a doleful look toward Jenny. "We're ruined if our herd is all dead. That's a lot to think about. I know I should be helping you, but all I want to do is sit here and worry. Getting out of a chair is an effort this morning. You and I have been fighting the good fight for a long time and I don't know how much I have left to give," she lamented.

Jenny was having none of Flannery's self-pity. She waved the spatula through the air in disgust and turned back toward the stove.

Boone sat down across from Flannery. "I didn't sleep, either. I was so wound up from last night. I should have gone after Joseph as soon as he got out of jail. That was my mistake. This just cannot continue."

"What are you going to do?"

"I haven't figured that out yet. I've played a hundred scenarios out in my brain, but I'm not sure any of them make sense. I just can't go murder him. Sheriff Stout would throw me in jail for sure and a grand jury wouldn't be scared of me."

Jenny carried the eggs, bacon, and biscuits over and set them in the center of the table. "That's a powerful man you're fixing to go up against. You best not get yourself killed. That won't do anybody any good."

"Especially me," Boone joked.

Flannery reached out and grabbed a biscuit. "There is nothing funny about any of this. Let's eat and then go see the damage."

As Jenny scooped eggs into her plate, she said, "You need to quit feeling sorry for yourself. This is the hand that God has dealt us and we need to deal with it."

"Why are you being so hard on me?" Flannery whined.

"Because you've never been a quitter in your whole life, but you're acting like one now, and I don't like it. We have to carry on or Jimmy's death will have been in vain. Flannery, we've been through tough times way back when and we got through them. You just need some faith that we're going to do it again."

Flannery slowly nodded her head. "You're right – you are always right. We need to figure out where we stand with our herd and go from there. No more complaining from me – I promise."

Boone and Jenny exchanged glances, and the old woman winked at him. He wished he shared her determination. In truth, he felt closer to Flannery's despair than he did Jenny's resolve. He just didn't see a way to win without getting himself killed in the process, and being dead wasn't going to do much good for him or the ranch.

As they ate the meal, Jenny tried her best to bring some levity to the situation, but received little reward for her effort. Boone looked too tired to find humor in much of anything she said, and while she had managed to get Flannery to quit feeling sorry for herself, the woman appeared to be a bundle of nerves.

"You two go on and get out of here before I sweep you out with the dirt. You're about to get on my last nerve. Savannah is the only one I have trained proper around here," Jenny warned.

Boone smiled and nodded his head. "I'll go get the horses saddled. Jenny, if you'd fix me a pie, my mood might improve considerably."

"If you want anything sweet, you'll have to get it from Flannery, but right now, her lips don't look too sugary to me."

Letting out a cackle, Boone said, "Well, you finally got me to laugh. See you later." He tipped his hat at Jenny and took his leave.

"The older you get, the more audacious your behavior. I never know what's going to come out of your mouth these days," Flannery complained.

"You better worry about what's coming out of my hand. I could still turn you over my knee if I had to. Any more whining out of you and that's what I'm liable to be doing."

Appalled by the comment, Flannery shook her head and headed toward the bedroom to change into her clothes. When she reemerged, she headed straight out of the house without saying a word in hopes of not further antagonizing Jenny. She came out of the house as Boone walked out of the barn. He was leading the two saddled horses.

"Well, it looks as if the sun is coming up today just like yesterday. Let's hurry up and get there so I can put myself out of my misery," Flannery said.

The couple took off at a lope toward the valley. When they reached the lip of the basin, they pulled the horses to a stop and gazed down below them. Ten head of cattle were lying on the ground, either dead or mortally wounded.

"Well, that's not as many as I feared," Boone said.

"This makes me sick. What kind of a person kills poor old dumb cows just to rile his neighbors? Please go put the live ones out of their misery. I can't bear to look at them," Flannery said.

Boone pressed his horse into moving down into the valley. He found three of the cows were still drawing breath, but beyond any chance of survival. As Boone shook his head in disgust, he drew his revolver and quickly put a bullet into the brain of each of the suffering animals. "You can come on down," he hollered.

Flannery joined him, and looked around one last time at the carnage. "Let's go see if we can find the herd," she said in a voice drained of any emotion.

As they rode out of the other side of the valley, they found three calves that had been trampled in the stampede. Seeing the crushed bodies proved to be the final blow for Flannery. Tears rolled down her cheeks and a couple of sobs escaped her that she failed to stymie. Boone tried to find some words to comfort her, but she held up her hand, silencing his attempt as they continued riding.

A child could have followed the tracks of the cattle. The grass was smashed down as if it had been cut. Boone and Flannery traveled for about a mile before they found the herd huddled together on a flat stretch of the ranch.

"Let's circle them and see if we see any more injured head," Boone suggested.

Flannery moved her horse without reply. They rode around the herd in silence without finding any maimed cattle, and stopped back where they had started.

"There's nothing lucky about this, but it could have been a lot worse. You can survive this," Boone said.

"Excuse me if I don't celebrate," Flannery said coolly. "I'm sorry I said that. That was uncalled for. You're right. I was expecting to be ruined. I should be grateful even if I don't feel like it at this moment."

"There's good grass right here. I say we leave the cattle where they are. They don't need any more stress with trying to move them."

"I agree. What now?"

"I want to ride to the river and see if I can find any signs that I shot any of the culprits."

Flannery waved her hand through the air. "Lead the way."

Boone led Flannery to the hill where he had first spotted the intruders. After looking around, he followed the tracks to the river where they disappeared into the water.

"I didn't figure I hit any of them. It would have been blind luck if I did. I could barely see them at that distance," Boone said.

"You tried. That's all you could do. I bet you put a scare in them anyway," Flannery replied.

"Let's go down and sit on those rocks there."

Flannery climbed down from her horse and marched to the rocks by the river's edge. She took a seat and watched as Boone came to join her on an adjoining rock.

"So what do you want to talk about?" Flannery asked.

"Who says I want to talk at all?"

Flannery rolled her eyes and glanced toward the river.

"Are you going to be all right?" Boone asked.

"Yes, I'm going to be fine. Compared to the day my sister, Josie, died, or the day that Jimmy was murdered, this is nothing. I admit that I overreacted, but I worried we were ruined, and with all that we've been through lately, this just became too much. I am sorry. I need to apologize to Jenny, too."

"You don't have to apologize to me. I think you handled things pretty well, all things considered. These are some trying times and can get to the best of us."

"I suppose so. Is Joseph going to win?"

Boone leaned over so that his shoulder touched hers. "Not if I have anything to say about it. I still don't know how I'm going to do it, but I'm going to put a stop to this. I may die in the process, but I swear to you that Joseph will die with me."

Flannery laid her head against Boone's shoulder. "Don't go getting yourself killed. I don't think I could take another death. Do you think I should just give up?"

"You and I probably don't have much in common at all, but the one thing we do share is that neither of us are quitters. We wouldn't be here today if we were and we're going to see this through."

Flannery raised her head up and smiled. "I hoped you would say that," she said. She leaned over and kissed Boone on the lips. "You are a bit of an acquired taste, but you are sweet – at least Savannah thinks so."

"I would talk. When I first met you, I thought you were permanently mad at the world."

"Maybe not permanently, but definitely mad at the world."

"I guess I have Savannah to blame for this mess I'm in. If she hadn't taken a shine to me on that first day, I probably wouldn't be here right now."

"That's true. I was ready to send you packing until you picked her up and quieted her down. I knew then that you had to be good. Someday, when she finally gets mad at you over something, I'll have to remind her that's it's all her fault that you're still around."

The couple laughed and then fell silent as they watched the river flowing by them. Minutes passed, while both were content to relax in the solitude and not think about what had happened or what lie ahead.

"I guess we better get back. Jenny will be sending out a search party," Flannery finally said.

"Boy, that woman doesn't cut you any slack."

"That's one of the disadvantages of living with a person your entire life. She knows exactly what I need, whether I want to hear it or not. And she could care less that I don't want to hear it. I love that woman."

"Let's get going then. I imagine Savannah is wondering where you are."

"She's probably more concerned with your whereabouts than mine. I have to be her mother. You're her plaything," Flannery said with a touch of envy in her voice.

"Savannah does have admirable taste in men," Boone joked as he stood.

The couple mounted their horses and turned for home.

While they were riding, Flannery asked, "So, do you miss being a gambler?"

Boone thought about the question a moment before responding. "You know, I thought I would, but things have been so hectic around here that I've barely given it any thought. I know you find this hard to believe, but I was good at cards. I still can't believe the run of bad luck I had. Maybe it was destiny to make me end up here."

"Maybe, it was, or maybe you're still on a bad streak."

As the house came into view, Flannery was the first to notice two horses in the yard. "Oh, my God, somebody is at the house," she cried out. She kicked her horse into a gallop and was gone.

Boone managed to spur his horse enough to catch up with Flannery. He drew his revolver as they raced into the yard and yanked their horses to a hard stop. The sudden arrival of the couple caused the two men standing there to turn their attention away from Jenny toward Boone and Flannery. Boone didn't know either man, but feared one of them was Joseph Thurgood. He pulled the hammer back on his gun and pointed the weapon toward them.

"Put your gun away. That's Wendell and Austin Starr," Flannery said.

"Are you sure I should? I didn't think they were your friends either," Boone said.

"I didn't say they were my friends, but I don't think they plan on killing us." Flannery felt a rush of embarrassment that the conversation had happened right in front of the men.

When Boone holstered his Colt, Wendell said, "Thank you, Flannery. I wasn't in the mood to get shot today."

"What do you want?" she asked.

"I had some of my herd killed last night. Your colored woman said you had the same done to you."

"She's not mine and her name is Jenny. She's part of my family."

"Oh, well, Jenny it is then. I didn't mean no offense by that. I'm truly sorry for my poor choice of words. I didn't come here to offend anyone."

"Surely you didn't think we killed your cattle," Flannery said. She climbed down from her mount to carry on the conversation.

"No, of course not. How many did you lose?"

"Ten cows and three calves."

"I lost thirteen and five."

"I'm sorry for your loss, same as I am for myself. You still haven't answered why you're here."

"Let me do some proper introductions first. I'm Wendell Starr and this is my son, Austin," Wendell said to Boone. He shook Boone's hand.

"I'm Boone Youngblood." Boone proceeded to shake Austin's hand.

"The reason I'm here is that I had a hunch that Joseph probably came after your cattle last night, too. Joseph has become a dangerous man. It's time to put a stop to him. Boone has quickly earned a reputation for being good with a gun with his killing of Hunter and for holding Joseph and his men at bay. I wanted to see if he'd be willing to help us put an end to this predicament."

"Wendell, why should we trust you?' Flannery asked. "For all I know, you could be planning on luring Boone away from here just to kill him. You certainly never treated Jimmy and me any better than Joseph did."

"I fully admit that I never welcomed you here like I should have. It irked me to no end that Jimmy bought this ranch out from under my nose when I didn't even know old McGregor was thinking of selling the place. I might have been a poor neighbor, but I swear to you that I didn't have a thing to do with Jimmy's death. I always suspected that the killer was Joseph, but I have no proof of that. I've bought two ranches lately, and have all the land I need now. Whether you help or not, I promise from this day forward to be a good neighbor. I'm getting old and it's time I changed my ways – and that's the truth."

Flannery looked toward Boone. "What do you think?" she asked.

"I like the odds of this a whole lot better than I do just sitting around waiting for something to happen. There is strength in numbers."

"What is your plan?" Flannery asked Wendell.

"I'll let Austin explain. As you know, he fought in the war. This is his idea."

Austin had stood quietly the whole time, but the bickering between his father and Flannery had made him nervous. In an attempt to keep from scratching his face, he rubbed the back of his neck and shifted his weight from foot to foot. "All of our men will ride to Joseph's home just as they're starting their day. We'll demand payment for the cattle. Joseph, being Joseph, will lose his temper and guns will be drawn. We'll be on horses. When the shooting begins, they will have to worry about getting shot and ran over by horses, all at the same time. If Mr. Youngblood is with us, it will be our ten men to their seven. It's a dangerous plan, but we have the odds," he said.

"Doesn't sound like much of a plan to me," Flannery said.

"We're open to a better idea," Wendell said. "But short of ambushing them in cold-blooded murder, it's the best we could come up with. Sometimes it would be more convenient if Sheriff Stout wasn't such a stickler about the law."

"It's a better plan than anything I came up with for going it alone," Boone added.

With a stoic look, Flannery glanced toward Boone. The thought crossed her mind about how the hand of fate in some poker games had led him here and could now possibly get him killed. She was ready for the madness to end, but she surely didn't want to do it at the cost of Boone's life. As the silence grew uncomfortable, she realized that she did not possess the wherewithal to make such a dire decision that could jeopardize his life.

Boone, sensing Flannery's dilemma, said, "I'm in. When do we do it?"

The question brought a smile to Wendell. "I like your grit. I figure we'll wait a few days in case they have their guard up for what they've done so that they aren't expecting a visit."

"Just let me know the night before," Boone said.

"I will." Wendell shook Boone's hand and then Flannery's. "To a new day of neighborly relations."

"To a new day," Flannery said.

Chapter 22

On Saturday morning, Boone had breakfast with the family before making a quick departure for the bunkhouse to clean his guns in anticipation of the coming showdown with Joseph and his crew. Flannery and Savannah were still sitting at the table while the child took forever to eat as she struggled to cut her flapjacks. After Flannery finally noticed her daughter's predicament, she began chopping the food into bites as Jenny returned to the table and sat down. Flannery glanced up and knew immediately from the black woman's expression that some momentous conversation was about to take place.

"What is it?" Flannery asked, sounding mildly annoyed.

"Me and Savannah are going to town so that you can have a private talk with Boone," Jenny replied.

"What? I don't think you need to be going to town alone."

"Not even Joseph Thurgood is going to bother an old black woman and a little white child right now. We'll be fine."

"I still don't have a clue as to what conversation I need to have with Boone."

"Boone is my friend," Savannah offered up.

Jenny rolled her eyes and shook her head at Flannery. "Boone is going to risk his life for us, and there's a good chance he could get himself killed in the process. I shudder even to say those words 'cause I've come to love him, but they are true. And if it were to come to pass, that boy deserves to go to his grave knowing how you feel about him."

The turn the conversation had taken so surprised Flannery that she pulled her head back and wrinkled her forehead. "Just because you caught us getting a little kissy doesn't mean that it was anything more than a couple of lonely people in a weak moment that took some comfort in each other. You blew that way out of proportion."

"Flannery Vogel, I've known you all your life. Do you really think old Jenny is buying what you're selling?"

Flannery narrowed her eyes and pursed her lips before replying. "All right, Jenny, the truth of the matter is I don't know how I feel about Boone."

Jenny gave her best motherly stare and let the silence hang in the air for effect. "Don't you?" she finally asked.

"Boone is my friend," Savannah repeated.

Flannery shoved a bite of flapjack into her daughter's mouth to silence her. "Jenny, I've known him for such a short time. How do I know if it's anything but loneliness? I'm only human, and it sure is nice to have the company of a man around here again. I don't trust my feelings."

"Well, at least now you're being honest with what you think, but are you really confused about your feelings or are you just plain old scared of them?"

Flannery let out a sigh so loudly that Savannah's eyes got big and she looked curiously toward her mother as she worked to chew the oversized bite that had been shoved into her mouth.

"Sometimes your meddling ways are purely annoying. I was perfectly content just to let this play out and see what happened. Now you make me feel guilty that Boone could die not knowing where he stands with me when I don't know for myself. And I can't stand the thought of another death around here. I think I would just wilt away to nothing if that were to happen," Flannery cried out.

"Sounds like you care a lot about him to me."

"Of course I care a lot about him, but that's not the same thing as wanting to spend the rest of my life with him."

Jenny began tapping her fingers on the table in a jaunty rhythm. "I was sure I knew how you really felt. Flannery, I'm sorry I upset you. I guess even I get things wrong once in a while."

Flannery smiled and her eyes welled with tears. She covered her mouth with a hand for a moment to gather her resolve. "Who am I kidding? I know how I feel, but I have such guilt about it that it's hard for me to accept it. What would Jimmy think? I am a widow after all, and here I am falling in love with his best friend."

"I knew it. I just knew it. I'm always right. Honey, Jimmy is gone. You can't think that way. And knowing Jimmy the way I did, I know he would hope that you were happy. Jimmy would have never wanted you to spend the rest of your life alone. And one more thing – Jimmy was so excited about the coming of that little thing sitting there beside you. In your wildest dreams, could you think of a better man to take his place for her?"

A hiccup sound escaped Flannery as she tried to catch her breath without breaking into crying. "Thank you, Jenny. You always know what I need to hear whether I want to hear it or not. Sometimes it makes me want to knock your head off, but I guess that's the price I pay for getting a dose of your honesty."

Jenny made a toothy grin. "You're not the only one that would like to make some heads roll around here every now and then. You need to go fix your face while I wash the syrup off Savannah. She's so sticky that the ants will be after her."

Flannery went off to wash her face and change into her clothes. When she returned to the kitchen, she waited there until Jenny and Savannah emerged from the back bedroom wearing their Sunday best.

"I'll help you get the wagon hitched," Flannery said.

"We're going to have a big time in Trinidad. If I can't spoil this child, well then, there's no point in living," Jenny said. She followed Flannery out the door.

Boone sat in front of the bunkhouse while he cleaned his guns. He spotted the women walking to the barn, and based on Jenny's outfit, figured she was going to town. After carefully setting his Colt onto the table, he headed for the barn to help hitch the horses to the wagon.

"Where are you going all dressed up?" Boone asked. He took the collar from Flannery and placed it over the horse's head.

"Savannah and I have some shopping to do. We need to get away from Flannery once in a while to keep our sanity," Jenny replied with a grin.

"I wish I had somewhere to go, too," Boone joked.

Once the team was hitched to the wagon, Jenny wasted no time in saying her goodbyes and leaving with Savannah.

"I'm going to go finish cleaning my guns," Boone said.

He was surprised when Flannery walked with him to the bunkhouse. She sat down in the chair next to his and watched as he resumed his task. Having her watching him made Boone self-conscious as he meticulously went about his task. For the life of him, he couldn't imagine how Flannery, with her busy-bee nature, didn't have something better to do with her time.

Flannery fidgeted in her seat as she tried to work up the nerve to start talking. She almost convinced herself that it should be Boone's place to begin the conversation about their relationship, but quickly came to the realization that by the nature of the situation, she was the one that needed to broker the subject. No matter how much Boone had become a part of the fabric of the family, she knew that he wasn't going to take things any further than a kiss without a signal from her.

"Are you worried about going after Joseph?" Flannery asked.

Boone looked up from his work. "You know me – I'm not a believer in worrying about something before it happens. I just plan to be ready and then let the cards play out," he said and shrugged.

"Well, it makes me nervous. I can't imagine this place anymore without you being a part of it."

"Well, I plan on coming back, but you were getting by before I was here and you'll be fine if I'm gone. You'll be able to hire some men after Joseph is gone. I haven't been here long enough to make that much of a difference anyway. Shoot, you'd probably forget all about me in time." Boone looked up and grinned as if he was trying to pass his comment off as a joke.

Flannery reached over and put her hand on his arm. "Boone, I'm never going to forget you – that's a promise. Finish cleaning your guns and then we need to talk."

"Oh, sounds serious."

Boone ran the cleaning rod down the barrel of the Colt until he was satisfied the steel was spotless. He reassembled the gun and loaded the chambers. "All right, I have both guns cleaned now. What's on your mind?"

Flannery leaned forward in her chair and took a deep breath to fortify her nerves. "I think we need to talk about us before you go try to stop Joseph."

Boone's first thought was that the time was at hand to start worrying. He'd been perfectly content to be patient to see what became of him and her. When Flannery had kissed him at the river, he'd felt sure that she had feelings for him. Now, he prepared himself to hear that things must come to a stop. "If this is about me kissing you out by the corral, I'm sorry. I just got carried away in the moment. I realize that you have a daughter to think about."

"No, that's not it at all. You've misunderstood what I meant. I'm just going to be blunt. There's a chance you could die when you go to fight Joseph, and I don't want to chance that happening without you knowing how I feel about you. Well, if I'm being totally honest, Jenny was the one that was worried about it and she got me to worrying about it, too," Flannery said and laughed nervously. "Boone, I love you."

Boone got a chill and could feel the goosebumps pop out on his arms and neck. He sat there tongue-tied with a blank look upon his face. He'd never been in love before now and had never said those words to a woman. In fact, he'd never let himself think about Flannery in that way. The notion that he could fall in love with her, and she not him, had scared him to death. As the silence grew awkward, he looked her in the eyes. "I love you, too."

Flannery exhaled loudly. "You scared me there for a moment. I thought you were going to say that you didn't." She laughed again nervously.

"What do you suppose Jimmy would think?"

"Jenny feels that Jimmy would be happy for us. I have to believe she's right. Life is for living and must go on. I hopefully have too many years of living left to have his death be where my life stopped being meaningful for anything besides being Savannah's momma. Jimmy wasn't the least bit selfish, you know that."

Boone had no idea on what to do or say. Never had he expected this conversation. He now knew why Jenny had been in such a hurry to depart for Trinidad. His head felt woozy as if he'd drunk a little too much whiskey.

Flannery leaned over and kissed Boone on the lips. The physical contact brought him out of his stupor and he kissed her back. Much like their day at the corral, they began a passionate embrace.

As they continued to kiss, Flannery thought of leading Boone into the bunkhouse, but something about the notion seemed tawdry as if he wasn't fit for taking to the house. She stood and grasped Boone by the hand.

"Let's go to the house," she said.

As they walked toward the home, Flannery had to squeeze her lips tightly shut to keep from laughing. Her fearless cowboy followed her like a meek little lamb. It seemed to her that sometimes the absurdity of life was too precious not to enjoy. She led him into the house toward the bedroom. When she reached her doorway, she paused. The moment was not lost on her that by crossing that threshold she was both metaphorically and physically about to begin a new chapter of her life.

Summoning up her courage, she marched into the room and embraced Boone.

The couple stood there kissing for a long time until Boone decided that Flannery must have been waiting on him to proceed any further. To his way of thinking, she had to be signaling to him that the time had come for him to take the lead. Emboldened by the revelation and his needs, he pulled her down onto the bed.

Boone made true love to a woman for the first time in his life. Afterward, as he rolled onto his back, he was amazed at the difference between what he had just experienced and his previous trysts with whores. He forced himself to temper the urge to shout out something stupid.

Flannery snuggled up to him. "I do love you," she said.

"And I love you. Before today, I wouldn't even let myself think about that. I was willing to wait and see what happened. I guess I couldn't imagine you loving me."

"I was willing to wait, too. We have Jenny to thank for the fact we ended up in bed together."

The couple laughed and then grew quiet, content to be in each other's arms.

"This brings a whole new meaning to cleaning your gun," Boone blurted out.

Flannery laughed and slapped his chest. "You're a naughty man. You know, it will be a long time before Jenny and Savannah get home. We have plenty of time to make sure we polish off any rust we might have missed the first time."

After the couple made love for a second time, they fell asleep in each other's arms. Flannery awoke from her nap with a start, fearing that Jenny and Savannah could be returning home at any minute. She jumped out of bed and began searching for her pieces of clothing.

"Boone, you need to get up and get out of here. Jenny doesn't need to know about this, and I sure don't want Savannah running in here and catching us naked," Flannery called out in a panic.

Boone sat up in bed and bent down to fish his pocket watch out of his pants. "It's nearly noon. I guess we plumb wore ourselves out with all that loving."

"You can brag about your conquest to me later. Get dressed. If Jenny finds out, I'll never hear the end of it."

Once Boone was dressed, Flannery gave him a kiss and all but shoved him out of the bedroom. "I love you, and I hope you understand why I want to keep this quiet for the time being."

"I love you, too, and I completely understand. I'll think I'll go check on the herd."

"That would be good. I think I'll fix a lunch for Jenny and Savannah. I expect them home at any minute."

Boone went into the kitchen and cut off a chunk of bread before heading out of the house. He ate his meal as he walked to retrieve his guns at the bunkhouse, stopping at the well to get a drink. After saddling his horse, he rode toward the pasture at a lope. He felt more free and alive than he had in ages. Never in a million years would he have guessed the day's turn of events. He grinned as his mind kept repeating "Boone Youngblood is in love."

Flannery combed her hair before going into the kitchen and retrieving boiled salt pork from the pan of water that Jenny had left it in to soak. She began frying the meat for sandwiches. Just as the pork started to sizzle in the pan, she heard the front door open behind her and turned to see who had entered.

Jenny came into the home with Savannah asleep on her shoulder. "So how did it go?" she asked. When Flannery involuntarily glanced down to the floor, Jenny knew all that she needed to know. "For goodness' sake, I told you to tell him how you felt, not show him."

"Jenny, hush. You don't know what you're talking about."

"Flannery Vogel, you couldn't lie worth a darn when you were a little girl and you still can't. Don't be trying to pull the wool over my eyes."

"Oh, all right, but you got what you wanted so I don't want a lecture."

"I never said I wanted you to take your knickers off for Boone."

Flannery put her hands on her hips and made a defiant pose. "Don't be crude. He and I are two adults after all. What did you expect would happen?"

Jenny shifted Savannah from one shoulder to the other and patted the child's back. "I surely didn't expect you to go loving on him as soon as you told him how you felt. Here I always thought you were a bit of a prude, and now I find out you are a little hussy. I worried about Boone going to his grave not knowing how you felt, but now if that were to happen, he'll be going there with a big ole smile on his face."

"Don't make light of such things. You'd be just as devastated as I would be if something happened to Boone."

The smell of pork starting to burn caused Flannery to turn to the stove and pull the pan away from the heat.

"Yes, I would, but my, my, my, today has surely been eventful. I'm going to put Savannah down and change my clothes," Jenny said before whisking away toward the back of the house.

Jenny put Savannah into her bed and looked up at the ceiling as if she was gazing at the heavens. "Dear Lord, I didn't exactly get my prayers answered as I expected, but sometimes it's better to receive more than less." She let out a giggle as she pulled off her dress.

Chapter 23

Boone declined to go to church with the family as he had on every Sunday since he'd been on the ranch. He ate breakfast with them and then hitched the horses to the wagon so that they could be on their way. After that, he piddled about until he felt certain that the family had traveled out of range of hearing his gunshots. He set some cans up and practiced shooting with his Colt. A long time had passed since he'd last used a revolver, and he went through a box of shells before he was satisfied with his draw and aim.

When the family returned home, Boone followed them into the house and sat down on the floor to play with Savannah while Flannery and Jenny made lunch.

As Flannery peeled potatoes, she glanced over at Boone and Savannah. Her daughter had Boone rocking a doll in his arms while she did the same with a second baby. The sight brought a smile to Flannery, and she nudged Jenny so that she would see it, too. Savannah certainly had him wrapped around her finger.

While Flannery watched them play, she realized that she knew so little about Boone. He remained a man of mystery to her. In fact, she didn't even know how she had managed to fall in love with him, but she certainly had.

Jenny hollered, "You're going to ruin your reputation as a notorious gunman if anybody were to see you."

Boone looked up and smiled. "That's fine by me. After this week is through, I hope I never have to be a gunman again."

"He just wants to be your lover from here on out," Jenny whispered to Flannery.

Flannery nudged Jenny with her hip and gave her a scowl. She'd made Jenny promise to act as if she knew nothing of the lovemaking, figuring the news would embarrass Boone to death. Knowing Jenny the way she did, she still worried that the old woman would make some sly reference to what had happened.

By the time the meal was prepared, Savannah had crawled into Boone's lap, forcing him to keep her engaged in conversation to prevent her from falling to sleep.

"Let's eat," Flannery announced.

After everyone was seated and the food had been passed around, Jenny looked at Boone and asked, "So what are you going to be doing for the rest of the Lord's Day?

"I thought I would take Savannah for a horse ride. She hasn't been on one since all the trouble started," Boone answered.

"Are you going to take Flannery with you?"

"She can come if she wants to. I'm sure not going to try to stop her."

"I believe I will ride with you," Flannery said.

"I bet she's good company," Jenny said with a grin.

Boone wrinkled his brow, puzzled by the comment. He also noticed that Flannery didn't look any too pleased with Jenny's remark. "She's fair to middling, but a whole lot nicer than when we had our introductions in the barn," he said, smiling at the memory.

"Maybe you're the one that made her nice." Jenny shot Boone an innocent-looking grin.

At that instant, Boone realized that Jenny knew all that had gone on between Flannery and him. "You told her?" he asked Flannery, astonishment in his voice.

"I never said a word. The old witch knew as soon as she looked at me. There certainly are some disadvantages to having known her all my life. I made her promise to keep her mouth shut, but you can see how long that lasted," Flannery said.

"I never said a word about what went on around here," Jenny protested.

"Honestly, Jenny, couldn't you have played fair for me?"

Jenny continued with her innocent-looking smile.

Boone leaned back in his chair and began tapping the fingertips of each hand together. "Well, Jenny, now that everything is out in the open, do you have anything that you would like to say about the matter?"

"I think the world of both of you, and I trust you'll both do right by each other. I can't say that I'm surprised by the turn of events or really even disappointed for that matter – maybe just shocked at the speed of things."

"So, in other words, this isn't to share your disapproval or anything like that. You just wanted me to know that you knew."

"I tried to keep my promise to Flannery, but you were too clever and figured me out. Anyway, it's not good for a family to have secrets. Now get to eating before your food gets cold."

Boone and Flannery locked eyes. Flannery raised her arms with her palms turned upward as if to say, "What are we going to do with her?" Boone, with a twinkle in his eyes, shook his head before taking a bite of mashed potatoes.

Jenny stayed on her best behavior for the rest of the lunch. Once they finished eating, Flannery offered to help with the dishes, but Jenny shooed her out of the house so that Savannah could get to take her ride before a nap. Boone was ready to spend some time outside to enjoy the day and was happy to have Jenny speed along things. He lit a cheroot he'd been saving and snatched up Savannah to carry her to the barn to saddle the horses.

"Go fast," Savannah said as they rode out of the barn.

"Maybe later," Boone said, putting his horse into a trot.

"Let's ride to the river, if you don't mind. Savannah can get her feet wet," Flannery suggested.

"Sounds fine to me."

After a leisurely ride to the stream with Savannah talking the whole time, they plopped down on the bank and pulled off their shoes. Flannery took Savannah by one hand, and Boone took the other as they began walking in the water's edge. Savannah was delighted by the new experience, and would rake her foot across the water, sending a cascade of drops flying through the air.

"So are you ever going to tell me anything about your past?" Flannery asked after a few steps.

Amused by the question, Boone asked, "Are you worried you might need to notify somebody after I cross paths with Joseph?"

"No, I swear to you that that never crossed my mind. You'd better come back all in one piece."

"To answer your question, probably not. There is nothing there worth telling."

"But you've obviously been around children a lot."

"All I can say about that is that I know that I don't have any of my own."

Flannery shook her head. "All right, I'll quit asking questions. I just don't understand why you want to be so secretive."

"You don't talk much about your past either."

"That may be true, but I certainly don't keep it a secret, either. I'll try to answer any question you may have."

"Nah, I have no reason to pry and it would make me a bit of a hypocrite, too, don't you think?"

"Well, you are a man, after all," Flannery teased.

After they walked for a while, one of Savannah's kicks to the water went awry and drenched the leg of Boone's pants.

Boone scooped up the child. "I'm going to throw you in the river," he teased.

"No, no, no. Don't," Savannah pleaded.

"What should I do with her, Mommy?" Boone asked.

"Throw her in the water."

Boone acted as if he was going to throw Savannah. She let out a scream and looked as if she was on the verge of crying. As soon as Boone saw her face, he felt terrible. He hugged the child tightly. "I wasn't really going to throw you in the water. I was just teasing. I'd never hurt you."

The words of comfort were enough to convince Savannah, and she wrapped her arms around his neck.

Boone tapped his index finger on his cheek. "You better give Boone a kiss so that he knows that you still love him," he said.

Savannah dutifully kissed his cheek, prompting Boone to smirk at Flannery.

"Let's go finish our ride," Flannery suggested.

After mounting back up, they rode to find the herd to show to Savannah, and then headed home. When they got back to the house, Boone and Flannery exchanged puzzled glances when they spotted Wendell and Jenny sitting on the porch, drinking coffee and laughing.

"Jenny is quite entertaining," Wendell said.

"So that's what you call it," Flannery said.

"We're paying Joseph a visit in the morning. Are you still in on this?" Wendell asked Boone.

"I am."

"Good. Glad to hear it. We'll meet you at the end of the road leading to Joseph's place at sunup. Any questions?"

"Just give me the directions."

Chapter 24

By the time that the gray of early morning gave way to light, Boone was waiting for Wendell at the end of the road leading to Joseph's place. Ten minutes later, the sound of horses coming from around a bend signaled the arrival of Wendell and his men.

"Good morning," Wendell greeted.

"Let's hope so," Boone replied.

"Yes, for sure. Before we ride in there, I want to go over a couple of things with you and my men. There's a chance that Joseph will pay for the damages. I doubt that happens, but if it does, we'll take our money and leave. I won't be part of murder. At least he'll know that now we're working together. That might be of some help to you and Flannery. The other thing is that the last time I was here, we all pulled our guns on each other but nobody fired a shot. Today, if one of them goes for his gun, let them have it. We are not here to play. Anybody have anything to say?"

"Please be careful," Austin pleaded. "This will be a battle."

Wendell pressed his horse into moving and the men followed him up the road. As the house came into view, men could be seen scurrying about the place in preparation for their day of work. One of the ranch hands spotted the oncoming visitors, and by the time the riders reached the yard, Joseph and his crew were huddled together to wait the arrival.

"What do you want?" Joseph asked, his tone menacing.

"This here is Boone Youngblood from the Vogel ranch. We've come for restitution for the cattle you and your men slaughtered of mine and theirs," Wendell replied.

Joseph looked Boone over, sizing up the man that had killed his son. "Are you a half-breed, boy? You look like one to me. I think I got a whiff of Injun, too. They always smell like buffalo breath."

"Today, I'm a debt collector," Boone replied.

Joseph laughed. "Let's hear you talk some Injun for us."

Boone smiled. He'd been taught long ago to never show anger in the face of your enemy. No matter what Joseph said to him, he would not be riled into a rash action. The one thing he was certain about was that his first bullet would be into Joseph Thurgood no matter if it cost him his own life or not. If he had to die, he'd go knowing that Flannery's troubles would be ended and that he had avenged Jimmy's death.

Wendell moved his horse up a step. "Let's get back to business. Joseph, we know you killed our cattle. There's no point in denying it. You should have plenty of money to pay us since you didn't get to buy the Cruft place."

"You arrogant old son of a bitch. I have no idea what you're talking about concerning your cattle. You need to leave right now."

"Or what?"

"Or I might have to shoot that halfwit son of yours."

"Joseph, I'm begging you to reconsider. We're not leaving until we are paid. Do you really want a fight?"

"You've been a thorn in my side ever since I started ranching. I'd take no better pleasure than killing you."

"Give us the damn money," Wendell demanded.

"See you in Hell."

Joseph grabbed for his revolver. His action caused a flurry of movement and sound as men reached for their weapons. Just as Joseph's gun cleared the holster, the roar of Boone's Colt signaled the end of any further debate. The shot slammed into Joseph's chest. Before he could react to his wound, a second shot from Boone took the rancher to the ground.

"Charge," Austin yelled.

As bullets started flying in every direction, Austin spurred his horse into the middle of Joseph's men. The former cavalry soldier looked as if he'd returned to the war he'd fought in all those years ago. He spun his horse in one direction and then the other as he fired off rounds. Two of Joseph's men were felled by his shots.

A shot caught one of Wendell's men in the neck. He dropped from his horse with his severed jugular vein shooting a fountain of blood.

The barrage of gunshots caused the air to thicken with a cloud of smoke of the black powder, making a pungent aroma in the still morning.

Austin spun his horse again and took aim on another ranch hand. Before he could shoot, two bullets found him simultaneously and he slumped over the neck of his horse.

With men scurrying about the yard, and horses jumping and bucking, Boone had a hard time taking aim on any of the men. Another of Wendell's men took a bullet. His horse bolted and slammed into Boone's mount, nearly knocking down the animal. As Boone rebalanced himself in the saddle, he saw a ranch hand taking aim at him. The two men fired at the same time. A wave of searing heat burned through Boone's thigh. He looked down and saw the blood darkening his pant leg. The shooter had dropped to his knees from the wound he'd received and was taking aim on Boone again when Calvin dropped him with a shot.

Elliot looked around at the carnage and panicked. He ran toward Wendell, firing his revolver with each step. As Wendell took aim on Elliot, he felt a pain in his side. He managed to shoot his gun anyway just as Calvin and Boone also shot at Elliot. The young man dropped to the ground and writhed in pain.

Joseph's remaining two ranch hands dropped their weapons and held their hands up in the air.

"Don't shoot us. We surrender," one of them called out.

Wendell slid down from his horse, and while holding his side, he ran to his son. Calvin joined him, and the two men pulled Austin from his horse and stretched him out on the ground.

Austin opened his eyes and winced with pain. "Looks like it's finally over with," he whispered. "All the hurt is going away. Pa, I can see the angels coming for me. Please don't cry. I'm at peace for the first time in years." He closed his eyes and slipped away.

The screams of pain coming from Elliot were joined with Emma's shrieking as she ran out of the house toward her son. She dropped to her knees and began tending to Elliot's wounds.

Boone eased himself down from his horse. His leg hurt like hell and he felt dizzy. He sat down in the grass and fetched his kerchief from around his neck to apply pressure to the wound. As Boone looked around at the carnage before him, he realized that at least two families would never be the same again. Wendell had lifted Austin up into his arms and was crying over the body. Joseph Thurgood was dead, and his son looked to be in bad shape. And some of the other dead men, of which Boone didn't even know their names, surely had loved ones somewhere, too. Boone just wanted to go home. He tried getting to his feet, but dropped back onto his butt as the dizziness got the best of him.

"Wendell, how badly are you hurt?" Calvin asked.

The question brought Wendell out of his grieving. He reached under his coat to probe his wound. "The bullet just grazed me. I think maybe I have a cracked rib," he replied.

Glancing around the yard, Calvin determined that he needed to take charge of the situation. He turned toward Joseph's two surviving ranch hands. "Go hitch up a buckboard wagon if you want Elliot to have a chance to live," he ordered.

The two men jogged toward a shed.

"Emma, which doctor do you use?" Calvin asked.

Emma looked up with a blank stare as if her mind no longer functioned. "Dr. Walsh," she finally answered.

"Wilson, go find Logan and tell him to head to Dr. Walsh's office."

"Yes, sir. I'll ride to his place right now," Wilson replied.

"Bobby, go to the Vogel ranch and tell Flannery to go to Dr. Smith's place. Make sure she knows that Boone looks to live."

Once Joseph's men returned with the buckboard, Elliot and Boone were lifted into the back of the wagon.

Calvin walked over to Wendell. "Let's get you to the doctor and let him check your ribs."

"I'll be fine. Horses have hurt me worse than this. I'm taking Austin home. Please get the men to put him across his saddle," Wendell said.

"Are you sure?"

Wendell nodded.

Calvin motioned with his head for the men to help him with Austin's body. After they had Austin secured to the saddle, Calvin helped Emma into the back of the wagon to be with her son. He tied his horse on behind the buckboard before climbing up into the seat. "Get Bill and Ketchup's bodies tied to their horses and then ride home with Wendell," he ordered the remaining men of the Starr crew. With a pop of the reins, the wagon headed for town.

Elliot's screams soon gave way to silence as he slipped into unconsciousness. The bumps in the road caused Boone to grimace in pain and grab his leg. He gritted his teeth and kept quiet.

"So what happened?" Emma finally asked.

Calvin looked over his shoulder at the distraught woman. "The other night, your men killed some of our cattle and some on the Vogel ranch. We came today for restitution. Joseph went for his gun and all hell broke loose."

"The damn fool always thought he was invincible. He cost me one son and now he may cost me a second. And Wendell lost poor, suffering Austin. I hope Joseph rots in Hell."

"I'm sorry things had to come to this."

"There wasn't anything any of us could do to stop Joseph. God knows I tried, but he just got more irrational with each passing year."

Emma grew silent and didn't speak again for the rest of the trip. Calvin pulled the wagon in front of Dr. Walsh's place and recruited some men to carry Elliot into the office while he escorted Emma inside the building. He quickly departed to go see Dr. Smith.

"Thank you for your help. You did a fine job," Calvin called out over his shoulder.

"It would have been a lot finer if I hadn't gotten shot," Boone said in an attempt at levity.

"I'm surprised there weren't more casualties. I think when Austin shot Fred Coup and Milton Frank, he might have saved several of us. Those were the two that knew how to fight."

"I'm sorry you lost Austin."

Calvin nodded his head as the words sunk into his mind. "Me too. Back when we were young, he used to be so different. You wouldn't have known he was the same person. At least his suffering is over with now. Wendell and my wife are going to take it hard."

"I sure hope this is the end of the troubles."

"I think it will be. I'm going to go see the sheriff and tell him that Joseph went for his gun and that I don't know who shot first. That's my truth and I suggest it be yours if you are asked."

"Sounds about right to me. If Joseph didn't die, others would have."

"Yes, they would have. Probably you and the widow for sure."

They came to a stop in front of the doctor's office. With Calvin's support, Boone limped into the building. When the doctor saw the bloodied visitor, he rushed to Boone's side and assisted in getting him up on the table.

"I'm going to go. I'm sure Flannery will be here shortly. You take care of yourself. I'll check in on you in a day or two," Calvin said.

"See you around."

Calvin left the wagon where it sat and walked to the sheriff's office. The sound of the door closing caught Sheriff Stout's attention and he glanced up from the wanted posters he was perusing. He did a double take as he realized that Calvin's shirt was drenched in blood.

"Oh, hell, what happened now?" the sheriff asked.

After dropping into the chair in front of the sheriff's desk, Calvin asked, "Do you have any whiskey around here?"

The sheriff reached into his drawer and retrieved a bottle and two glasses. After pouring generous amounts, he slid one of the drinks across the desk. "Drink up," he said.

Calvin took a drink and savored the taste a moment before swallowing. He needed one more sip before relating the day's events and what had led to the battle.

Sheriff Stout let out a whistle when Calvin finished his story. "I knew Joseph would get himself killed one of these days or I would hang him. Are you telling me the truth on everything?"

"I am." Calvin took another drink of whiskey. He felt more nervous now that he had spoken than he did beforehand.

"Since you took all your men with you, I'm guessing you were expecting a fight?"

"We were, but Joseph had plenty of opportunities to pay us and prevent trouble. When he went for his gun, all bets were off."

"Do you think Elliot will live?"

"He might if he didn't lose too much blood. He was hit in the arm and hip."

The sheriff took his first sip of whiskey, and leaned back in his chair. "I'll have to talk to him and everybody else that was there."

"That's fine by me, but I swear to you that Joseph was the first one to reach for his gun."

"I believe you. That certainly sounds like Joseph. You need to get on home. Wendell and Kelly will be needing you. I'm sorry about Austin. You know, as troubled as he was, I always had a fondness for him. I fought in that war, too, and I know what he went through."

"Thank you, Sheriff Stout. I'll be seeing you."

Calvin tipped his hat and walked out of the office. The thought of telling Kelly that her brother was dead made him want to visit a saloon rather than go home. Instead, he walked to the wagon and retrieved his horse.

Chapter 25

Flannery burst into the doctor's office with Savannah in her arms and Jenny at her skirt tail. The doctor turned his attention away from Boone to look over his shoulder at the new arrivals. Unperturbed by the sudden intrusion, he managed a faint smile.

"Hello, Flannery. We've been expecting your arrival," Dr. Smith said in a wry tone.

As Flannery gulped a deep breath before speaking, she reminded herself to stay calm. "How badly is Boone hurt?" she asked, her voice sounding shaky nonetheless.

"I had to sedate him to remove the bullet from his thigh. He should be waking up shortly. All things considered, for a gunshot wound, it is not a bad injury. No bones were hit. Just some muscle damage. Your man should make a full recovery as long as he's a good patient. He'll need plenty of rest and to take it easy. If he does too much and rips the wound open, he's liable to get blood poisoning. I'll be making a one-legged dancer out of him if he does."

Flannery and Jenny dropped into adjoining chairs at the same time. The rush of relief they felt seemed to have taken their legs out from under them.

"Boone is sleepy," Savannah noted.

"Yes, he is, honey."

"Can we take him home?" Jenny asked.

"Sure. We'll keep him here until the anesthesia wears off some. He might feel sickly. Jenny, I'll send some iodine and carbolic acid home with you to flush the wound with," the doctor replied.

"Don't you worry yourself about him getting rest. I'll tie that boy to the bed if I have to. He liked to have scared us to death," Jenny said.

"I wasn't aware that you had a man on the ranch. I've never seen him before today. Where did he come from?"

"He was Jimmy's friend. They served together in the Texas Rangers," Flannery answered.

"He seems like a fine fellow. We had us a nice little conversation before I put him to sleep. There seems to be a whole lot more to him than your average ranch hand."

Flannery grew flustered, and hesitated to respond, wondering whether Boone had said more than he should have in his pain.

"We've grown right fond of him," Jenny said to end the lull. "Savannah thinks he's about the best thing since candy."

"Speaking of which," Dr. Smith said. He walked over to his desk and retrieved a sucker that he handed to the child. "Let's all relax and wait for Boone to awaken."

Twenty minutes passed before Boone began to stir and another hour went by after that before he could talk coherently. He did provide some humor in the meantime when he told Flannery that he sure would like to dance with her and asked Jenny to teach him to sing.

"You weren't supposed to get shot," Flannery reminded Boone.

"Austin died," Boone replied quietly.

"Oh, that's terrible. I feel for Wendell. He's going to be lost without having Austin to take care of."

"I feel bad for Mrs. Thurgood, too. Joseph is dead and Elliot is in bad shape. I doubt he lives. That'll be two sons in about a month."

The doctor walked to a closet and selected a pair of crutches from inside it that he judged would be the right size for Boone. He brought them over to his patient. "You are to use these to go back and forth to the table to eat and not much more than that. If you don't take care of yourself, you could still lose that leg or your life. Do I make myself clear?"

"If you lived with these two women you'd know that there will be no chance that I would disobey orders. Renting a cell at the jail would probably be less confining."

"I wouldn't be too hard on them. They were about consumed with worry when they rushed in here for you."

"They were just worried about losing their laborer. They about work me to death," Boone teased.

"Boone Youngblood, people go to Hell for lying. You took a good ten years off my life today, and I don't have that many more left," Jenny said.

"I was really just talking about Flannery. When I get well, you and I just might strike out on our own," Boone replied with a wink. He winced as pain surged up his leg.

"You'd better get him home. He won't be quite so full of himself later on. He's going to be in pain. I only prescribe a willow-bark tincture. Laudanum kills more people than the injuries it treats," Dr. Smith said.

As Dr. Smith helped Boone swing his legs off the table, Sheriff Stout walked into the office.

"Looks like you're going home," the sheriff said.

"I am unless you plan on arresting me."

"I'd like to hear your side of the story if you feel like talking."

"Sure. Have you checked on Elliot yet?"

"I have. He's in bad shape. Dr. Walsh had to take off most of his right arm. If he lives, Doc thinks he'll need a cane or crutch to walk for the rest of his life, too. Emma acted so hysterical that the doctor had to sedate her."

Boone nodded his head solemnly before recounting the gunfight nearly identically to Calvin's telling.

"Well, you take care of yourself. I'll be in touch," Sheriff Stout said.

With Flannery and Jenny each holding onto Boone's arms, he managed to use the crutches to get to the buckboard. He sat down on the end of the wagon and scooted himself forward with considerable effort and pain.

"Send for me if you need me," the doctor said.

"Thanks, Doc. I'll be a good patient, I promise," Boone said as Flannery popped the reins and made the horses lurch forward.

The ride home about took the last of the starch out of Boone. He let out a couple of yelps when the wagon hit bumps, and when they pulled into the yard, his shirt and forehead were covered in sweat.

"Let's get you in bed before you pass out," Flannery said.

"I bet you rue the day you found me in the barn."

"Nonsense. You're just tired and in pain. Come on."

Boone labored to make it to the house. When he got into the front room, he used the crutches to support his weight as he stopped to rest. He felt dizzy again and needed to suck in air to clear his head.

"He can have my bed," Jenny offered.

"No, we'll put him in my room," Flannery said.

"And where will you sleep?"

"Where I always do. I can keep an eye on him this way. It's a double bed and I'd rather sleep with him than share it with you and listen to you snore. I'd never get any sleep."

"I just bet you would. Flannery Vogel, you're not setting much of an example for your daughter." Jenny put her hands on her hips and gave her a motherly look.

Boone stood there watching the two women argue. He hurt too much and felt too weak to care where he slept or who won the battle. The notion that he might be sharing a bed with Flannery didn't even interest him. He only wished that they would hurry up and make a decision.

"For goodness sakes, she's only two. She doesn't understand any of this and she surely won't remember anyway. Now let's get Boone to bed before he collapses while we stand here and argue." Flannery gave Jenny a look that dared her to speak.

"It's your house and you're the boss," Jenny said in a hurt tone.

They helped Boone to the bedroom and got him comfortable. Flannery pulled a chair up to the bed with the intention of staying with him until he fell asleep while Jenny went to fix some food for them.

Once Boone's breathing sounded relaxed, Flannery couldn't resist the urge to lean over and kiss his forehead. The ride into town that day had felt like the longest trip in her life. She had convinced herself that they would find Boone dead, and if not for Jenny's faith that he would be fine, she doubted she would have had the strength to walk into the doctor's office. A sudden urge to cry overcame her, causing her to bolt out of the room and into the kitchen as Jenny scooped oatmeal into bowls.

"I just didn't have it in me to cook a proper meal," Jenny said.

"I understand that. It's been a long day already," Flannery replied.

After they carried the bowls to the table and were eating, Jenny blurted out, "We could have lost Boone."

Flannery glanced up and studied her friend. Jenny looked old and tired. Her forehead was etched with concern and her eyes lacked their usual merriment. Flannery decided that the time had come for her to be the strong one. "I know we could have, but he's going to be fine. Quit your worrying."

"I know, but it brings back memories of when we lost Jimmy. I don't believe I could have stood another loss like that."

"Jenny, try to think of happier things. We are safe now thanks to Boone and Wendell."

Jenny nodded her head, but she needed to talk things out before she could move on. "I feel so bad for poor Austin. That man never had much of a life and now he's gone. I wonder why he couldn't get past the war."

"I guess some things are just too terrible to forget."

"But you moved on after Josie and Jimmy died."

"I might have moved on, but I certainly never got over them entirely. I just experienced their losses while Austin was a part of all kinds of deaths of men I'm sure he cared deeply about. I would imagine that he felt guilty over some of that and maybe even guilty that he survived and they didn't. That's a lot to bear."

"That's all true, I suppose. I feel bad for Wendell, too."

"I need to pay him a visit. I certainly owe him that."

Jenny nodded her head and took a bite of oatmeal.

Savannah was being unusually quiet, so Flannery looked over at her daughter. The child had fallen asleep as she ate. "Wouldn't it be nice to be so carefree that you could fall asleep at the drop of a hat?"

"Yes, it would. Speaking of carefree, if you get to loving on Boone, you're liable to kill him."

Flannery dropped her spoon into her bowl, causing Savannah to jump but not wake. "Would you please let that go? There isn't going to be any loving – I can assure you of that. My goodness, Boone will be lucky even to sit up in bed for a few days. You're being ridiculous."

"The sitting up isn't the part that worries me. You play with matches and you're going to get burned."

"Honestly, Jenny, just eat your oatmeal so that I don't have to listen to your nonsense."

∞

Calvin had gone home to deliver the news of Austin's death to Kelly. His wife had cried until she vomited. His daughters, Sally and Renee, were hysterical over the news. Nothing Calvin said brought any comfort to any of them, and he stood by helplessly as they grieved. When Kelly had finally gained some measure of composure, the couple, along with their daughters, headed to the home place in a buckboard wagon. When they arrived at the ranch, they found Wendell and the ranch hands making coffins.

At the sight of her father, Kelly jumped off the wagon and ran into his arms. She hugged him and began sobbing again. Wendell patted his daughter's back and mumbled some words of comfort.

"Aren't you going to take Austin to town to the undertaker?" Kelly finally asked.

"I was going to and then I got to thinking about how your brother hated crowds or a fuss made over him. I thought that maybe we would just have the family together to bury him. Of course, if you disagree, I'm willing to do what you think is best," Wendell replied.

Kelly stood there and chewed on her lower lip as she mulled over a decision. "No, I think Austin would have preferred just the family to be there. Where is he?"

"We have him in the house, but I haven't cleaned him up yet. You might want to wait."

"No, I want to get him ready. I know the suit I want him buried in. Calvin can help me, and the girls can stay out here with you. They need you right now. I can do this."

"I think that's a fine idea, but prepare yourself for what you're about to see," Wendell said and hugged Kelly again.

Calvin and Kelly walked into the house and found Austin laid out on a table with a tarp under him. The sight caused Kelly to catch her breath and clutch her chest.

"Do you want to be alone with Austin?" Calvin asked.

Grabbing her husband's hand, Kelly said, "No, I want you right beside me."

A flood of memories came rushing back to Kelly as she willed herself to stroke Austin's hair. Her brother was five years her senior and had always been such a sweet and shy boy, but so overprotective of her. Nobody messed with Austin Starr's little sister. She had always been amazed that Calvin had been persistent enough to court her with all of Austin's attempts to end their romance. The two boys had been friends their entire lives, but nobody measured up enough for Kelly in Austin's book.

"Godspeed, Austin," Kelly said, and wiped her tears away with her sleeve.

∞

As the time neared five o'clock, Logan and Dr. Walsh finally convinced Emma that there was nothing she could do for Elliot and she should get on home to get some rest. Logan helped his mother up onto the buckboard and tied his horse behind the wagon before heading for home.

"Your father really did it this time," Emma said once they had ridden out of town. "He finally got himself killed and Elliot maimed for the rest of his life if he does live."

"Yes, he did. I don't know what he was thinking. Was Pa always this way?"

Emma stared straight ahead at the road as she shook her head. Tears began running down her cheeks, and Logan had to hand her a handkerchief so that she could blow her nose. "No, he wasn't at all. I had the choice of several suitors and I would have never married Joseph if I'd known he'd turn into such a fool. He was so sweet and thoughtful back then. Over the years, he just kept getting greedier. I don't know why. We didn't want for anything. You know that."

"I'm going to stay here and run the ranch."

"No, Logan, you can't. You've finally broken free from this place. You were going to escape. This is your time. We'll be fine."

"Elliot wouldn't have been able to run the ranch even if he hadn't gotten hurt. He's not mature or smart enough. You know that. He might not even be able to ride a horse after today. My mind is made up. We've all put too much of our lives into that ranch to let it all go to hell now."

Emma burst into sobs. "You're such a good son. I don't know what I would do without you. I would have gone crazy a long time ago if I didn't have you to talk to," she said.

The rest of the ride was traveled in silence. When they reached home, the sound of hammering drifted out of the barn. Logan pulled the wagon up and saw Pete and Nick nailing the lid onto a casket they'd fashioned.

Nick walked out of the barn to meet them. "I'm sorry for your loss, Mrs. Thurgood. How is Elliot?"

"Thank you, Nick. Elliot is still alive, but that's about it," Emma answered.

"We made coffins for everybody. Pete thought it would be a good idea to make one for Joseph to take him to town in, too. We would have brought him on in, but we didn't have the wagon."

"Right now, my only concern is Elliot. We'll bury everybody in the family plot. Logan knows where Joseph and I are to be buried. He can show you in the morning. I don't have time to worry about a wake."

Logan glanced over at his mother as he contemplated trying to change her mind, and then thought better of it.

"Would you like to see Joseph? We haven't nailed his lid down," Nick said.

"No, I wouldn't. I saw him this morning in all his dead glory. I just want to get into the house. Maybe in the morning."

Logan walked his mother into the house and got her settled before fixing her some scrambled eggs. They even managed to have a laugh about the eggs. Scrambled eggs were the first thing that Logan had ever learned how to prepare, and he would find any excuse to make them until Joseph had gotten concerned he was raising a future chef instead of a rancher. After Emma finished eating, she retired to bed.

After pouring a glass of brandy, Logan took a couple of sips to fortify himself before walking to the barn.

"So did Pa have all of you go kill Wendell and Flannery's cattle?" Logan asked. He could see that the question caught the two men off guard and they stood there looking down at their boots. "Come on, guys. I just want the truth. I know you were just following orders. I'm in charge now and I intend to make things right."

"We did," Pete answered.

"Was Pa the first one to draw his gun today?"

Pete nodded his head.

"The sheriff will be coming to get statements from you two. I want you to tell the truth. Both of you have been loyal to this ranch and I appreciate that. Go on to the bunkhouse and fix something to eat. I want some time with Pa."

Once the men had left the barn, Logan slid the top off his father's coffin. The sight of the once thunderous man, now still and pale, jolted his senses. Joseph still wore the blood-soaked shirt he'd died in. The blood and the smell of death caused a wave of nausea to course through Logan and he nearly bolted for the door.

"You won the battle to keep me on the ranch. I have to hand that to you, but you most certainly lost the war. You went and got yourself and others killed for pure foolishness. Elliot is maimed for life. I'm going to run this ranch the proper way and be a good neighbor. I hope that galls you to no end in Hell."

Having said his piece, Logan returned the lid back onto the coffin and walked to the house to finish his brandy.

∞

After supper, Flannery made chicken broth for Boone. She carried a bowl of the soup into the bedroom and found him sitting up in bed. Boone looked to be feeling better, too. His color had improved and his eyes no longer looked pained.

"I wasn't expecting to see you up. You were really sleeping away a little while ago," Flannery said. She gently placed the tray onto Boone's lap.

"I've been on my back about all I can stand for the time being. I had to sit up," Boone replied.

"And how are you feeling?"

"Better than when we got home. If you and Jenny had argued any longer, I would have just stretched out on the floor at your feet." Boone gave Flannery a beguiling smile.

"I'm sorry about that. Jenny can be so opinionated. Sometimes, I think she believes she's still my boss."

Boone took his first bite of broth. "Oh, this tastes so good. I was starving. You and Jenny have a lot of history. That's always a double-edged sword."

Flannery tried smiling, but her emotions got the better of her. She put her hand to her mouth to stifle a cry, but the sobs escaped her anyway. "You scared me so badly today. When we learned you were shot, it brought back so many bad memories. I just don't think I could live through all of that again."

"Come up here and sit beside me."

Flannery climbed onto the bed and scooted up next to Boone.

Boone threw his arm around her. "I'm going to be fine. I promise to be a good patient, and I'll be up and around in no time. The trouble is over with. Joseph is dead and Elliot is crippled. They won't be trouble anymore. Heck, that ranch is now liable to go up for sale. And I take Wendell at his word that he'll be a good neighbor from here on out. I sure feel for him losing his only son. You could see he was crushed. Anyway, I think tomorrow will be a new day around here."

After Flannery leaned her head on Boone's shoulder, she asked, "Are you worried about the sheriff?"

"Nah, it was a fair fight. Even if they convene a grand jury, I don't think it will go to trial. We did nothing wrong. Joseph had his chance to pay up and avoid a fight. He chose wrong."

"Are you sorry you showed up here?"

"The only thing that I'm sorry about is that I didn't come a lot sooner."

"I love you."

"I love you, too."

Chapter 26

Once Sheriff Stout had interviewed all the men present at the gunfight, he came to the conclusion that Joseph Thurgood had been the culprit in starting the melee. For the sake of propriety, he decided to hand his findings over to the grand jury so that no one would accuse him of playing favorites. Two weeks passed before the grand jury reconvened, and when they did, they quickly agreed with his conclusions and chose not to prosecute any of those involved in the gun battle.

When the sheriff received notice of the findings, he decided to pay a visit to the three ranches involved in the shootout. He took a leisurely ride out of town and made his first stop at the Vogel ranch. As Sheriff Stout rode into the yard, he found Boone sitting on the porch with his crutches leaning beside him and Savannah standing directly in front of him while she sang a song. The sound of sheriff's horse caused the little girl to abruptly quit her singing and turn to see who was arriving.

"Looks like you have babysitting duties," Sheriff Stout called out.

"That's about all shot-up cowboys are good for. Flannery and Jenny are baking and we've been informed we're not welcome inside the house," Boone replied.

Sheriff Stout climbed down from his horse and walked up onto the porch. "You must be healing well or they wouldn't already be throwing you out of the house."

"That I am. I can bear weight on the leg now and plan to start using a cane as soon as my three bosses give me permission."

The sheriff laughed. "You're the one that chose to live in a henhouse."

"Yes, I did. All the attention is certainly better than getting ignored, but I have to go to the outhouse to be alone, and for the first few days, they accompanied me there, too."

Slapping his legs, Sheriff Stout got so tickled that he snorted while trying to catch his breath. "That's a good one."

"Have you heard how Elliot is doing?"

"He's home now. I saw Logan a couple of days ago and he said that the doctor wants Elliot to be up and moving around so his hip doesn't lock up permanently, but he just wants to stay in bed and mope."

"He's got a tough row to hoe. I do feel for him even if he was the enemy. He's just a son trying to please his daddy. Flannery paid Wendell a visit yesterday. She said he looks old and worn out. He was cordial to her, but she could barely get him to talk. I worry about him."

The sheriff took a seat beside Boone and began loading his pipe with tobacco. "Wendell is a tough old cuss. I think he'll be fine in time. He still has a lot to live for."

"I sure hope so. I'm not sure we would have survived if he hadn't gotten involved. The odds were certainly not in our favor."

"So what's the plan now?"

"We're going to hire a couple of ranch hands and get this place back into shape. Once we get things in order in a year or so, we're going to expand the herd."

"Sounds like you've found a permanent home."

Boone chuckled. "It seems I have. Can you believe I gave up the life of a gambler for this?"

"At least Flannery doesn't take your money."

"She hasn't given me very much of it either."

The two men laughed. Sheriff Stout struck a match and lit the tobacco. He puffed on the pipe until he had it burning to his satisfaction.

"Well, I think you're a welcome addition to our community. I came out here to ..."

Flannery walked outside. "I thought I heard voices and laughter," she said.

"Hello, Flannery. Good to see you. I was just getting ready to tell Boone that the grand jury decided there was nothing about the gunfight to take to trial," Sheriff Stout said.

Flannery covered her mouth with both hands and her eyes began to well with tears. "That's such good news. With the way things go around here, I was worried to death about that," she mumbled through her hands.

The sheriff glanced over at Boone and then back to Flannery. He had a sneaky suspicion that there was a lot more going on between the widow and ranch hand than just employer and employee. "Well, I need to pay visits to the Starr and Thurgood ranches, too. I don't want to keep you from what you're doing."

Dropping her hands to her side, Flannery said, "I'm sorry to be so emotional, but we've been through a lot. Thank you for coming, sheriff."

Sheriff Stout shook hands with Boone. As he turned to leave, he remembered the candy in his pocket. He reached into the bag and pulled out a piece to hand to Savannah. "Here is a piece of candy, little lady," he said.

"Thank you," Savannah obediently responded.

Boone got to his feet and braced himself with his crutches as he stood beside Flannery. They watched the sheriff ride away as Savannah chomped on the hard candy.

"This is a good day," Flannery announced.

"Yes, it is, but I wasn't really worried about the grand jury. You kept your angst hid from me," Boone said.

Ignoring the comment, Flannery said, "Do you feel up to walking out into the yard with me?"

"Sure."

Flannery scooped up Savannah and walked off the porch. She stood there until Boone joined her.

"Do you hear that?" Flannery asked.

Boone wrinkled up his face and tilted his head upward as he listened. "All I hear is the wind through the trees."

"Exactly. Jimmy used to say that that was our song. He said you could tell how happy a place is by listening to the wind. This is the best music I've heard in a long time."

Boone dropped the crutch on his right side and threw his arm around Flannery and Savannah. "I'd say it's the best I've ever heard. I hope to be able to come and stand here to listen to it for a long, long time."

"Me too."

"I believe the hand of fate has just dealt ole Boone some winning cards for a change."

Jenny walked out onto the porch. "I wondered where you all went off to. You leave me to do all the work," she bellowed.

Flannery turned her head. "The sheriff just left here and there won't be any charges over the gunfight."

"That's surely good news," Jenny said. She bounded off the porch to join the others.

"Yes, it is. Boone is healing up and our troubles are over. This is a wonderful day," Flannery said.

Jenny walked in front of the couple. "Speaking of Boone getting well, I ain't no fool. I know what's going to be happening, if it isn't already, and I won't have you two living in sin right in front of our baby. Savannah doesn't need to be under the same roof of such goings-on."

"Honestly, Jenny, no such thing is happening. You need to mind your own business for once," Flannery said.

"Boone, you've been nothing but an honorable man since you came here, but you tasted the candy and need to pay for the sweets and make an honest woman out of Flannery. You two need to quit dallying and get married," Jenny lectured.

"Oh, my goodness," Flannery uttered.

Boone grinned and rubbed his chin. "You know, Jenny, there's a whole list of things that need doing around this ranch. I just might have to put that on the list. We'll have to see when we can get around to it. That list is pretty long."

"Yeah, and old Jenny just might take charge of your list. You know I always get my way around here when push comes to shove."

About the Author

Duane Boehm is a musician, songwriter, and author. He lives on a mini-farm with his wife and an assortment of dogs. Having written short stories throughout his lifetime, he shared them with friends and with their encouragement began his journey as a novelist. Please feel free to email him at duaneboehm@yahoo.com or like his Facebook Page www.facebook.com/DuaneBoehmAuthor.